"You're a natural, Zoe."

She dropped her gaze to her feet and tucked a loose strand of hair behind her ear. "I love animals, especially dogs. Always have. They're forgiving and eager to please. I get them, and they get me."

"I can see why." He trailed a finger down her cheek.

Her eyes shot up, and he dropped his hand. Something flashed across her face, but before he could decipher it, she turned and headed for the front door.

"Thanks, Zoe. For everything."

She placed a hand on his forearm and squeezed. "My pleasure, Sully. I'm really looking forward to this."

"Me, too." He curled his fingers over his arm where her hand had been, to lock in the feel of her tender touch against his skin.

Maybe, by working together, they'd have an opportunity to revive the past connection they'd once shared. Maybe he could be the one to alight her eyes with joy once again. Would she ever give a broken has-been like him a chance?

Books by Lisa Jordan

Love Inspired

Lakeside Reunion
Lakeside Family
Lakeside Sweethearts
Lakeside Redemption

LISA JORDAN

has been writing for over a decade, taking a hiatus to earn her degree in early childhood education. By day, she operates an in-home family child-care business. By night, she writes contemporary Christian romances. Being a wife to her real-life hero and mother to two young-adult men overflows her cup of blessings. In her spare time, she loves reading, knitting and hanging out with family and friends. Learn more about her at lisajordanbooks.com.

Lakeside
Redemption
Lisa Jordan

HARLEQUIN® LOVE INSPIRED®

Recycling programs
for this product may
not exist in your area.

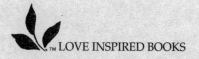

™ LOVE INSPIRED BOOKS

ISBN-13: 978-0-373-87934-2

Lakeside Redemption

www.Harlequin.com

Printed in U.S.A.

I have swept away your offenses like a cloud,
your sins like the morning mist. Return to me,
for I have redeemed you.
—*Isaiah* 44:22

For my mom who is a daily testament of God's redeeming grace. I'm so honored to be your daughter.

For my fairy godmother agent Rachelle Gardner and wildly talented editor Melissa Endlich—thank you for picking up the pieces and walking alongside me during the writing of this story. I couldn't have done it without you. I'm so blessed to have you on my writing team.

Acknowledgments

Thanks to the Love Inspired publishing team for helping me bring another story into print.

Susan May Warren & Rachel Hauck— thank you for answering the call of the pineapple and speaking truth into my life. You're amazing friends and the best mentors.

Carolyn Vibbert, Amanda W., Cathy West, Mindy Obenhaus, Michelle Lim, Reba J. Hoffman and Beth K. Vogt for your brainstorming, feedback and encouragement.

MBT Core Team, MBT Ponderers, Coffee Girls, Spice Girls and Sisters in Stitches for your words of encouragement and prayers that kept me going when I lost my way. I love you all!

Chandra Smith of Best Friend Dog Training—thank you for your dog training advice. Any mistakes are my own.

Pat, Scott, Mitchell— you are my anchors. I love you forever.

My Heavenly Father—You give me an endless supply of grace to endure the challenges that come my way. Thank You for loving me unconditionally. Thank You for redeeming me. I am nothing without You.

Chapter One

What was Caleb Sullivan doing in Shelby Lake?

Although Zoe hadn't seen Sully in ten years—not since the day he graduated from Bartlett University and headed off to the police academy—she would have recognized his smile anywhere.

Zoe pulled her pink Canine Companions baseball cap lower on her forehead and slipped her sunglasses back on her face.

Hopefully he wouldn't recognize her.

It wasn't that she didn't want to see him. She just didn't want him to see what she'd become. She fingered the blue-and-silver butterfly pendant hanging around her neck.

Holding hands with two little girls—his daughters, maybe—Caleb approached the Canine Companions booth centered in the middle of the park for Shelby Lake's annual Paws in the Park event.

Leona, her boss and owner of Canine Companions, had chosen the worst possible time to take a break from manning the booth and promoting her business while Zoe tried to stay in the background by overseeing the puppies. She hated being in the public eye, on display for everyone's personal scrutiny.

With the late-August afternoon sunshine at their backs, they stopped in front of Harper, her black-and-white border collie, who was sitting at her feet and watching the park activity. Her brother, Ian, and sister-in-law, Agnes, had given her Harper for her birthday last year.

Caleb glanced at her, then held out his hand and allowed Harper to sniff it before petting the dog's head. The older child did the same, but the younger one clung to his leg.

Zoe studied his dark hair threaded with silver, his hazel eyes and the shadow of a beard that did little to disguise his strong jaw. His navy V-neck T-shirt hugged his chest and displayed muscled biceps. Wearing faded jeans and a pair of running shoes, he bore a slight resemblance to the lanky guy she palled around with in college. The furrows above his brows and etched lines around his eyes and mouth showed this man had experienced life.

The older girl, who appeared to be about five, chattered like a hyperactive chipmunk. Dressed in an ice cream–stained yellow T-shirt, purple tutu and lime-green rain boots, with her blond hair pulled into a ponytail, she skipped over to the makeshift play yard where the puppies jumped and tumbled over one another.

Carrying the younger girl, Sully followed her and then knelt on the ground, a grimace tightening his face as he rubbed his right thigh. He wrapped his other arm around the smaller child wearing a denim skirt and multicolored flowered shirt while they watched the puppies.

The older child pulled on his arm. "Daddy, we need a dog. Avie thinks so, too. Right, Avie?"

Ava nodded.

"A dog?" He scratched his chin. "They need to be fed and played with and walked, Ella. I won't be able to do it all by myself."

"We could help you. Right, Avie?"

Ava nodded again.

Ella twirled and clapped her hands together. "Yay, Daddy. We can pick out a puppy today. Right, Avie?"

A look Zoe could only describe as fear crossed over the child's face. Her eyes ricocheted off Sully to the puppies. She buried her face in his shoulder.

He ran a finger over her cheek. "Hey, baby girl, maybe the nice lady will let you hold one of the puppies. Want me to go ask?"

She peeked out at the puppies, then at Zoe, but her older sister held no reservations. "Oh, yes, Daddy, please ask her."

Sully laughed, a rich, mellow sound that transported her back in time to a decade ago, when life held fewer complications.

His gaze locked with Zoe's. "Would it be possible for my daughters to hold one of the puppies?"

"Of course." Zoe smiled and stepped through the gate. She scooped up Riley, a caramel-colored, curly-haired cockapoo with a white patch around his left eye, and carried him outside the play yard to where Sully sat with his daughters.

Riley wriggled to be free and licked her cheek with his tongue, knocking her sunglasses at an odd angle. She laughed, trying to keep the wiggling puppy from jumping out of her arms. Her hat fell off her head but caught on her ponytail. She pulled off her hat and sunglasses and dropped them on the grass as she sat cross-legged in front of the girls.

Trying not to let Sully's penetrating stare get to her, Zoe focused on the girls and patted the grass next to her. "Want to sit by me? I'll show you how to hold Riley."

Ava glanced at Caleb. He nodded. "Go ahead, sweetie."

She clung to him for a moment, then crept over to sit next to Zoe.

"Hold your hand like this." Zoe held her hand, palm side down, in a loose fist in front of Riley's nose. He sniffed, then licked the backs of her fingers. "Riley will smell your scent and get to know you."

Ava mimicked Zoe's gesture with her tiny hand. Riley sniffed her fingers, then stroked them with his tongue. She giggled and wiped her hand on her shirt.

Zoe placed the puppy on Ava's lap and positioned her small arms around Riley so she could hold him without hurting herself or the puppy. A smile lit up Ava's face.

Ella plopped down next to her sister and wrapped an arm around her shoulder. "You're doing great, Avie. You like him?"

Ava nodded, but remained quiet.

Sully pulled out his phone and snapped a picture of the girls. Then he looked at Zoe. "Is Riley available for adoption?"

"Riley is a recent addition to our shelter." She reached behind her to grab a brochure off the booth and handed it to him. "This talks about our adoption policy, Mr....?"

Of course she knew his name, but since he didn't seem to recognize her, she wasn't going to let on she knew who he was.

"Sorry." He held out a hand. "Sullivan. Caleb Sullivan." His gaze zeroed in on her butterfly necklace. "That necklace...I've seen it before." Still holding her hand, his eyes searched her face as if shuffling through his memory bank for some sense of recognition. Then a slow smile spread across his face, revealing even, white teeth. "Zoe. Zoe James. It's been a long time."

Pulling her hand out of his warm, firm grip, she nodded, then focused her attention on the girls. She patted the grass beside her, feeling for her sunglasses and hat.

Did Sully know what she had become? Where she'd been? If he did, he hadn't let on. If he didn't, she was sure he'd want nothing to do with her once he learned about her past.

Apparently their friendship had meant a lot more to her than it had him. After his graduation from Bartlett University, he had packed his dinged Toyota, hugged her goodbye and never looked back. Not a single letter or email.

She'd heard through the grapevine he had married Valerie Fergus, who had graduated with him. What Caleb ever saw in that woman, Zoe would never know. From the moment Caleb started tutoring Zoe in algebra, Valerie had gone out of her way to give Zoe a hard time.

Were they still married?

She glanced at his hand. No ring, but that didn't mean anything. She'd learned long ago not to assume, given her own circumstances.

Sully moved next to her and stretched out his legs, blocking any attempt to stand and run. "How's life been treating you?"

How did she answer his polite attempt at conversation? An ache pulsed in the pit of her stomach. She fingered the butterfly pendant.

Life treated her the way she deserved.

"Fine." The trite words mocked her. She was anything but fine. "You?"

"You know..." His words trailed off as he shrugged. He picked up a fallen leaf already turning colors and twirled it between his fingers.

"Are you still in law enforcement?"

"No, at least not the way I was." A vacant look hollowed out his eyes as he stared past her shoulder and rubbed his right thigh. "Took a bullet to the leg that ended my career as a beat cop."

"I'm sorry." And she meant it. Becoming a police officer had meant everything to him. She understood the pain of lost dreams.

He shrugged. "It is what it is."

"What brings you to Shelby Lake? Last I heard, you were living near Pittsburgh."

"I decided we needed a fresh start. Patrick Laughton was an old marine buddy of my dad's, so I called to see if he had any use for a washed-up cop with a bum leg. Turns out the police department had an opening for a school liaison officer. I'll be going to the schools in the district doing programs on the dangers of drugs and alcohol. What about you? Did you end up going to vet school?"

"No. Change of plans." Her gaze shifted to his daughters showering Riley with attention. "Your daughters are darling."

"Thanks. We've had a rough year—first my injury, then their mom took off." A flicker of pain shadowed Caleb's eyes. "I heard about Kyle. I'm sorry for your loss."

Words clogged her throat as her heart thundered against her rib cage. "I'm sorry about your wife. What did you hear...about Kyle?"

"He was killed by a drunk driver. I should apologize for not coming back for his funeral." He nodded toward the daughter in the tutu. "Ella had just been born, and my wife, Val, had a hard time with postpartum depression. Between work and some…family issues, I had my hands full." He scrubbed a hand over his face and sighed. "I'm sorry. That sounded a bit insensitive."

"No…don't be." The knots in her stomach cinched tighter. She rubbed her empty ring finger.

A man and a woman holding hands walked past them. The woman also held a toddler's hand while the man controlled a golden retriever on a leash.

The epitome of family.

She wanted that…almost had it once.

Now she had nothing but the pain of regret, broken promises, and fines as a reminder of what her choices had cost her.

Even though she sat in the park surrounded by open spaces, the hills to the right of her seemed to be shifting and closing in. Her breathing quickened as beads of sweat broke out on her forehead.

Sully reached for her arm. "You all right?"

She blinked several times and ran a hand over her mouth. "Yeah, I…uh…I'm fine. Probably too much sun."

Liar.

She wasn't fine. She hadn't been fine in a long time. Not since she'd woken up in the hospital that night with a concussion and learned Kyle was dead.

The events of the past four years had destroyed everyone and everything she loved.

She reached up, grabbed her water bottle off the booth's table with shaky hands and uncapped it. As she downed the lukewarm liquid, she closed her eyes and struggled to regain her composure.

Leona wouldn't be thrilled if she freaked out in front

of a potential client. And she didn't need to give this town anything more to gossip about.

No, she wouldn't be fine for a very long time…if ever again.

But life had offered her a second chance, and she wasn't about to waste it on pity parties.

Now that she'd moved into her family's cabin by the lake, she was determined to get her life back on track. Watching Sully with his daughters created an intense longing in her heart and resurrected her purpose: to regain custody of her own child and prove to her family—and the town that rejected her—that she could change and be the kind of mother her son deserved.

Caleb was going to get kicked out of the neighborhood if that fur ball didn't stop barking.

He threw back the covers, pulled on yesterday's jeans and T-shirt and padded barefoot to the living room. Flicking on the lamp on the table next to the coffee-colored leather couch, he winced at the sudden brightness and shot a one-eyed glance at the clock hanging above the doorway that led into the dining room.

4:15.

He groaned and stretched out on the Berber carpet in front of the dog crate, which had become his new middle-of-the-night normal since bringing the little guy home a few days ago.

Riley looked at him with large, soulful eyes and whimpered.

"Hey, little man, some of us need to sleep." He pushed his fingers through the metal and scratched the dog's muzzle. Riley licked at Caleb's hand.

What had he been thinking? He didn't have time for a dog. They needed exercise and companionship.

He could handle a walk around the block, but his hiking and running days were over. Besides, he had his hands full caring for the girls. Now he had something else to take care of.

Rubbing the heel of his hand into one eye, he released the latch on the crate. Riley bounded out, searching for freedom.

Caleb scrambled to his feet, biting down on his bottom lip as pain shot to his right hip, and scooped up the pup.

Carrying him to the back door, he switched on the outside light and let Riley down. He scurried across the patio and sniffed the grass for the best spot to do his business.

Caleb dropped onto a white plastic yard chair and waited.

Stars sparkled against the early morning sky with soft light smudging the horizon. A hint of a breeze ruffled his hair and cooled his face. The Turners' house next to his corner lot sat in darkness.

At least Riley's barking hadn't disturbed them.

Having moved to Shelby Lake less than a month ago, he'd bought the one-story ranch with a large fenced backyard on a quiet residential street.

Once things settled down, he'd get to know his neighbors Shawn and Pam Turner. Maybe invite them over for a barbecue. They had a daughter a little older than Ella. Shawn was a fellow cop with the Shelby Lake Police Department, and Pam taught third grade at Ella's new school.

But first he needed to finish unpacking and get the girls' swing set assembled. Maybe they'd even like a swing hanging from the sturdy oak shading the patio. The yard called out for summertime picnics, roasting marshmallows over an open fire and running freely without having to worry about city traffic.

Down the road, once his heart healed from his ex-wife's betrayal and desertion, he'd consider finding someone who wanted those same things, someone who realized he was enough.

Maybe.

Right now, he was just too exhausted to think about sharing his heart again.

But that didn't stop Zoe James's face from flashing through his mind.

If he hadn't been so focused on the girls, he would have recognized her much sooner, especially with that butterfly necklace she never took off.

Once she realized who he was, though, she retreated inside a polite shell. For a few minutes, she laughed easily with his daughters. The sound of her laughter and the joy in her smile were exactly as he remembered.

No one else had those green eyes with glints of gold that wandered into his dreams every now and then. Eyes that touched his soul. Eyes belonging to his college roommate's girlfriend and Caleb's former secret crush.

Seeing her again unleashed a memory of another time, another place…a memory he didn't allow his mind to visit because the pain of that time nearly undid him.

She had gotten under his skin from the moment they met at Bartlett University during his junior year, when she had been a freshman needing a tutor in algebra. Despite the hours they shared in the library, she had fallen for his roommate when the twerp serenaded her like in some cheesy romantic movie.

Zoe's engagement to Kyle the same weekend he and Kyle had graduated had nearly ruined him, so he dropped all contact with her on purpose. Marrying Valerie on the rebound hadn't done either of them any favors. Focused on his law-enforcement career and his family, he'd lost touch with his college buddies as well.

That seemed like a lifetime ago, but seeing Zoe again stirred up a lot of memories, particularly the ones he had created with her, such as walking her back to the dorm after tutoring, celebrating her exam success with ice cream, and that night at the go-kart track after Kyle ditched her to go out with someone else behind Zoe's back.

Maybe he'd be able to get to know her all over again.

As friends.

Being new in town, he could use a friend.

Riley ran to Caleb, pulling him out of the past, and stared at him with eager eyes. Caleb reached down and lifted him, rubbing his furry head. "Good boy."

They went back into the house. Caleb snapped off the light and locked the door. He reached into a bag of dog treats and tossed one to Riley, who caught it and scurried under the coffee table to devour his snack.

Even though his eyes burned, he probably wouldn't be able to get back to sleep. He hadn't slept a full night in the past year. Nightmares or unexpected shooting pain often woke him out of a deep slumber.

Caleb headed for the couch and reached for his laptop, only to have the power cord come up short. He stared at the chewed cord, then at the pup whose muddy-brown eyes were the picture of innocence.

"Dude, really? I bought you a pile of chew toys. Why my cord?"

Riley rested his chin on his paws and whined.

"I get it, man. I do. You're lonely, too." Caleb set the

laptop on the floor and lifted the little bundle of fur out from under the table. "It stinks, doesn't it?"

Riley trembled in his arms and clawed at his T-shirt as he tried to crawl up his chest.

Why hadn't he waited until they were more settled to get a dog?

The delight on his daughters' faces as they played with the puppies at the Canine Companions booth had sealed the deal. After Valerie walked out on them, Ava had clammed up, refusing to speak. He missed her chirpy, chatty voice.

He'd lasso the moon out of the sky and serve it to her on a platter if it would help her speak again.

That's how he'd ended up with a puppy on his chest.

Caleb stretched out on the couch and readjusted the dog. Riley settled into the hollow of Caleb's neck, warming his neck with his puppy breath.

As he curled an arm around the little body, warmth flowed to Caleb's heart.

For a moment, the loneliness that was his constant shadow evaporated.

Why hadn't he been enough for Val? He had been committed to making their marriage work, even after he realized her dependency on alcohol came first in her life.

Maybe he should have tried harder to get her more help to stay sober.

She'd checked out of their marriage long before he ended up in the hospital, recovering from surgery after one bullet shattered his femur and another took out his partner during a drug raid gone bad. Valerie, the one who promised eight years ago to stay by his side in sickness and in health, deserted him and the girls for some idiot she'd met online.

He'd do whatever it took to create a stable home again, and help his daughters heal from their mother's abandonment. He'd make sure they knew they were enough.

The good news was the past disastrous year hadn't kept him from still wanting the Hallmark version of marriage and family.

Someday.

But right now he lay on the couch in a half-unpacked house with little girls who cried out for their mom in their sleep and a puppy that whined and chewed everything in sight.

He needed help.

It took a lot for him to admit that, but a twelve-pound fur ball had him licked.

Once daylight broke, he'd call Canine Companions and request Zoe's dog-training services, which he had read about in the adoption packet he received with Riley. The girls needed to know how to handle their new pup safely and with care. After all, how hard could it be?

And the thought of seeing Zoe rekindled a spark he thought had burned out. As he closed his eyes, memories tumbled through his thoughts. The way Zoe's eyes lit up when she laughed. The way she hid behind her chestnut-brown hair when she was embarrassed. The butterfly-shaped birthmark on the inside of her right wrist was another way she stood out from the other girls he knew.

His crush on her was so long ago. Besides, she probably had her life together and didn't need a train wreck like him crashing into it.

Riley scampered down the hall, his nails clicking on the laminate flooring. He ran back into the living room with one of Caleb's ties in his mouth. Of course it had to be an expensive silk one.

Caleb grabbed it out of his mouth, traded it for a rubber chew toy and carried the tie back to his closet. Halfway down the hall, he stepped in a warm puddle. "Riley!"

He made it to his room and fell forward on the bed, burying his head under the pillow.

He needed a hot shower, a heavy dose of caffeine, then he'd put in a call to Canine Companions.

Too bad there wasn't a service for broken single dads to help them come back to life after they'd lost everything.

Chapter Two

Working with animals reminded Zoe she wasn't a total failure.

"Fetch it back, Winston." She tossed the tennis ball over the German shepherd's head.

The dog bounded after it, his tags jingling on his collar, and returned with the ball in his firm jaws. She held out her hand. "Release."

Winston dropped it on her open palm.

"Good dog." She wrapped her arms around his solid neck and patted his fur. "You're such a good boy."

He barked, then licked her cheek with his coarse tongue.

For as long as she could remember, Zoe had preferred stuffed animals to dolls. As a child, she'd set up animal clinics and offer free checkups to her assorted teddy bears, unicorns and puppies.

She understood animals, especially dogs, and they understood her. They could look deep in her heart and see she was sorry for her actions. And they didn't continue to cast blame on her.

Working at Canine Companions gave her a sense of

fulfillment. Not only was she able to use her skills, but also she was getting paid to do something she truly enjoyed.

Canine Companions owner Leona Billings believed dogs were an important part of a family, and her center reflected her values. The bright, leash-free, doggie-daycare play area, with its tiled floor, climber cubes with steps and comfy cots, offered their canine friends plenty of socialization and free play as well as structured walks and exercise.

In addition to the doggie daycare, Canine Companions offered training, grooming and shelter for rescued stray or surrendered dogs, which were housed in the other building until they could be placed in their forever homes.

Today they cared for six dogs in the daycare— Winston, the German shepherd; Maisy, an aging cocker spaniel; a tiny Maltese named Emma, who arrived dressed in a pink dress covered in daisies; Penny, a black Chihuahua-dachshund mix, snoozing on one of the cots; Max, a black-and-white poodle mix and Earl, a Tennessee Brindle, who sprawled in front of one of the climbers, chewing on his rubber bone.

The door to the play area opened, and Travis, Leona's twenty-two-year-old son and Zoe's coworker, popped his head around the door. "Yo, girl. What's up?"

"Playing with the pups. How's it going with you?"

Dressed in a royal blue Canine Companions T-shirt and faded jeans with his long tea-colored hair pulled back into a ponytail, he moved into the room, closing the door behind him. Penny and Max rushed over to him. He scooped them up, one in each arm, before sitting cross-legged on the floor. "Going good. Ma wants a word. Got time to chat with her?"

"Sure. Can you hang out here with the dogs while I'm gone?" What could Leona want in the middle of her shift?

"Can do."

"Great." Zoe pushed to her feet, brushed off her jeans and bumped knuckles with Travis as they traded places.

She closed the door behind her, shutting out the barking, and followed the paw-print decals on the floor that led to Leona's office at the end of the hall. The scents of bleach and dog were replaced by coffee and cinnamon.

Zoe knocked on Leona's open office door.

Leona looked up from her laptop, smiled broadly and waved her in. "Hey, Zoe. Having a good morning?"

"Yes, they're an energetic bunch today, but it's all good. We're going for a walk in a bit."

"Great. Glad to hear it. Want some coffee or tea?"

"Coffee would be great, thanks."

Leona left her desk that was tucked in the corner of the room and crossed to the table near the windows. She poured coffee into an "I Heart Dogs" mug and handed it to Zoe.

She cupped her hands around the warm ceramic mug and tried not to feel like she had been summoned to the principal's office. Her mind raced, trying to think of different reasons why Leona wanted to talk with her. Was her job performance suffering? Was she being fired?

Her stomach knotted, and she forced her hands to remain steady. She closed her eyes and drew in a soothing breath. No sense in getting worked up until she had details.

Focus on something else.

Leona's office looked more like a family room with red-and-tan-plaid couches and matching chairs, end tables piled with dog magazines and a large-screen TV tucked in an oak cabinet used for training videos. Beige valances hung over large picture windows that over-looked the fenced-in backyard.

Not even five feet tall with an apple-shaped body decked out in a leopard-print blouse and matching shorts, with a shock of spiked purple hair, Leona had the kind-est heart in Shelby Lake. In the year Zoe had been em-ployed at Canine Companions, she'd learned Leona was a woman of second chances and fairness.

Her boss understood the need for redemption after serving time a couple of decades ago before she'd found God, a wonderful husband, and started her family. Except for her sons, all of the Canine Companions employees were people to whom Leona had offered a second chance. Her compassion kept them wanting to stay on as staff.

Leona refilled her own cup and carried it to one of the couches. She kicked off her sequined flip-flops, then tucked her feet under her tanned thighs, not one to stand on formality. Instead she embraced her staff as family—she was all some of them had.

She waved a hand for Zoe to sit. "I just got off the phone with a man who attended Paws in the Park last weekend with his family. He was quite impressed with the way you responded to his daughters."

Sully. Had to be him.

Zoe sat on one of the matching chairs next to the couch and melted against the cushions. The busyness of the day caught up with her as she sipped her coffee. "I didn't do much. I helped the girls handle the puppies safely."

"Don't sell yourself short, Zoe. You know your stuff when it comes to animals. I watched you with this fam-ily. So I'm glad he called and mentioned it, too."

"I appreciate his kind words. You could have sent me

a text or something. No need for a trip to the principal's office." She smiled to show the hint of teasing in her tone.

A throaty laugh burst from Leona's lips. "Having spent my fair share of time in the principal's office as a teenager, I can understand how you may be feeling, but rest easy. You're not in any trouble. In fact, I'm about to offer you a promotion."

"A promotion? Really?" She sat up and set her coffee mug on the table next to her chair. "But I haven't been here that long."

"You've been here long enough for me to see your potential. I believe what I'm offering will be a good fit for your abilities. As you're aware, Mr. Sullivan adopted Riley for his daughters. He's had the little guy for a few days now and it's chewing everything in sight. He'd like you to help them train the puppy."

The thrill she felt at Leona's initial mention of the promotion vanished. "Leona, as much as I'd love to help you, I can't."

The image of Sully's two girls playing with the puppies swirled into her thoughts, pulling out emotions she'd suppressed for a long time.

"Sweetie, there's no reason why you can't be around children. Besides, Mr. Sullivan said you two were old college friends. He asked for you specifically. Talk to him, tell him what happened so it doesn't come up later, then seriously consider taking the job."

Zoe reached for her cup and traced her thumb over the words on the mug. The desire to work with Sully and his daughters ballooned in her chest until she feared her lungs would burst. But once he learned the truth… "The minute he finds out about my past, he's going to take his pup and sprint in the other direction."

"You don't know that." Leona pulled off her red-rimmed glasses and used them as a pointer to punctuate her words. "You need to start having faith in people again, Zoe."

"Second chances in this town are about as real as the Tooth Fairy." She disliked the edge that steeled her words, but several encounters over the past year had proved her point more than once.

"Not everyone feels that way, Zoe. Give this family a chance." Leona scooted to the edge of the couch and slipped her feet back into her shoes. "Besides, wouldn't you rather your friend hear it from you rather than neighborhood gossips?"

"I guess."

Leona crossed to the window and peered outside. "Well, you have about two minutes to think about what you'd like to say because he just pulled into the parking lot."

Zoe stiffened as her heart bounced against her ribs. "Thanks for giving me time to prepare."

"If I had given you any more time, then you would've talked yourself out of doing it. Buck up, girl. You can do this. I believe in you." Leona placed a hand on her shoulder for a moment before heading for the door, leaving Zoe alone to stare at her reflection in the cooling cup of coffee.

A few minutes later, voices down the hall reached Zoe's ears. She set her cup on the table and stood, brushing the dog hair from her royal blue Canine Companions polo shirt. She didn't know why she bothered. Once Sully learned her story, he wouldn't want her services anyway.

She wiped her palms on her thighs as Leona ushered him into the room.

For a second he hesitated in the doorway, the breadth of his shoulders filling the space. He wore an unbuttoned blue plaid shirt over a gray T-shirt with the sleeves rolled up, exposing muscular forearms. His faded jeans rode low on his hips. Black Chuck Taylors completed his casual look.

Dear God, let him give her a chance.

When he saw her, a smile spread across his face. He ran a hand over his wind-tossed hair and walked over to her. He extended his hand. "Zoe, good to see you again."

"Thanks, you too." She shook his hand and forced herself not to reach out and hug him, which had been their usual greeting years ago. Times had changed. They were practically strangers now. And after today, she'd probably never see him again.

She motioned toward the couch. "Have a seat."

"Thanks." He lowered himself slowly onto the cushion. A grimace tightened his face.

She wanted to lend a hand, but Sully came across as the kind of guy who wanted help only when he asked for it.

Leona returned and handed a cup of coffee to him. "Here you go, Mr. Sullivan. I'll leave you two alone while I check on the kids."

"Kids?"

"My four-legged ones, of course."

"Yes, of course. And please call me Caleb."

Leona winked at Zoe, then scurried out of the room, closing the door behind her, taking Zoe's courage with her.

She didn't want to tell her story again, but if she wanted to work with his daughters, he needed to know the truth.

He set his coffee on the side table and leaned forward. "So Leona said you wanted to talk to me?"

"Yes." Zoe stood, hugged her arms to her waist and walked to the window that overlooked the dog play yard. Travis had taken the dogs out to splash around in the plastic kiddie pool.

She loved watching the pups cavorting with freedom. Closing her eyes, she breathed a prayer for her missing courage. Turning back to Sully, she opened her eyes and faced him. "Before you hire me, there's something you need to know."

Sully frowned. "What's up?"

Her heart picked up speed, and she wiped her damp palms on her jeans again. Then she shoved her trembling fingers into her front pockets. Tears filled her eyes as her voice dropped to a whisper. "I'm the one who killed Kyle."

Caleb shot to his feet. Surely he didn't hear her correctly? "What did you say?"

Her eyes pleaded with him as she shook her head. "Please don't make me say it again."

So there was nothing wrong with his hearing.

But he couldn't believe it. Wouldn't believe it. The Zoe he knew and loved at one time wouldn't hurt anyone.

Her words ricocheted through his thoughts, slicing through what he thought was his bulletproof sizing up of the woman from his past.

He rubbed the back of his neck. "Would you care to explain? I thought Kyle had been killed by a drunk driver."

She dashed a trembling hand across her mouth and tugged on the hem of her shirt. "Maybe you should sit."

With the weight of her words pressing him down, he slumped against the back of the couch and stared at her.

Zoe sat on the edge of the chair across from him. She bore little resemblance to the lighthearted girl from college. Right now she appeared weighted down with a burden too heavy for anyone to carry.

She cupped her knees and straightened her arms. Exhaling loudly, she raised her chin, trapping his gaze. "I partied a lot in high school."

He never did get into the drinking scene, even with his buddies on the force. Then after what he went through with Val… "I'm kind of surprised you didn't mention this years ago. Did you drink in college?"

"No. A friend of mine almost died at a party during my senior year. A group of us ended up getting arrested for underage drinking. After they bailed me out, my parents gave me a choice—get my act together and make something of my future, or they were going to send me away to some sort of reform school. I chose Plan A."

He never would have pegged Zoe as a party girl, but he knew all about appearances being deceiving.

His bones seemed to have melted under his skin, leaving him feeling weary and way older than his thirty-two years. He scrubbed a hand over his face, then looked at her. "What happened to Kyle?"

"On the night of my twenty-third birthday, Kyle and I went out with friends for a few drinks. I didn't want to. I hadn't slept well the night before, and I had worked all day. I was afraid if I started drinking, I'd end up down that same path, but Kyle insisted. That first drink tasted so good, and the second one went down even easier. Kyle kept pounding back shots and ended up wasted. I got into an argument with my brother on the phone about when we'd be back. He had been watching our son—"

Sully held up a hand. "Whoa. Slow down. You have a kid?"

Her eyes widened. "You didn't know?"

He shook his head. How would he?

Scarlet crept across her cheeks. "Yeah, I got pregnant my junior year of college. I left Bartlett to take care of Griffin. He's nine. And he's absolutely perfect. Nothing like his mother."

"So you and Kyle ended up getting married?"

The blush deepened. Zoe dropped her eyes to her lap and shook her head. "Kyle wanted to wait. Anyway, we left the club. Kyle was in no condition to drive. I truly thought I was okay. Otherwise I never would have gotten behind the wheel."

How many times had he heard that during his years on the force? Why didn't people get it? Even after one drink, they shouldn't drive.

"We were a block from my parents' house when a guy ran a red light and crashed into us. I hit my head and blacked out. I woke up in the hospital and learned Kyle was dead."

"You didn't know you were responsible?"

She shook her head. "I was unconscious and couldn't give consent for the blood alcohol test, but the officer on the scene suspected alcohol was involved. He subpoenaed my clinical blood test that the hospital had administered." She tucked a stray hair behind her ear and swallowed. "My blood alcohol content came back over the legal limit. I didn't cause the accident, but the prosecution argued my reflexes were diminished. Kyle's parents had a lot of money and could afford the best attorneys. They tried to use my past offenses against me."

"Your juvenile records can't be used against you."

"The judge ordered their remarks to be stricken from the records, but they succeeded in swaying the jury's opinion. I was found guilty of vehicular homicide while driving under the influence. I served four years at VWCI."

Vanderfield Women's Correctional Institute.

Caleb leaned an elbow on the arm of the couch and pressed his fist against his lips as he processed Zoe's words.

Not only had he witnessed his wife destroying their lives with her choices, but he'd spent years arresting people suspected of driving under the influence. He heard their excuses, their pleas, and listened to their lawyers argue in court in their defense. They deserved to be held accountable for their actions.

And now Zoe had just told him she was like one of those people he'd arrested more times than he could remember.

His beautiful Zoe with the eyes that peered deep into his heart. His beautiful Zoe with the laugh that allowed him to fall in love with her over and over again.

His friend was dead because of her decision to get behind the wheel.

He simply couldn't wrap his head around it.

No, not his beautiful Zoe.

He'd walked into Canine Companions hoping she could help him out with the wayward puppy probably eating his couch right now. He didn't expect any of this.

He leaned forward, braced his elbows on his knees and rubbed his hands together. "I'm not going to lie, Zoe, this has…thrown me for a loop. Man, I did not expect it in a million years."

"I understand." She stood and moved toward the door. "Thanks for coming in. I'm sorry it didn't work out."

"Hold up. I said it threw me for a loop. Sit back down. I'm not leaving just yet."

Zoe hesitated. She glanced at the door. A look he could only describe as yearning crossed over her face. Did she wish she could throw it open and run from the room?

"You were great with Ella and Ava last weekend at the park. I know they'd enjoy learning from you."

"But?"

He filled his lungs, then released the air in a long burst. "But the thing is, my ex-wife was an alcoholic who walked out on our marriage and our daughters to shack up with some guy she met on the internet."

"I'm sorry, Sully. I understand. I do. I'd love the opportunity to work with you and your daughters, but I get your hesitation. If it makes a difference, I've spent the past year at Agape House––a transitional home for women released from prison started by my family. I've been given a second chance, and I'm not going to mess it up this time. A couple of weeks ago, I moved into my family's cabin by the lake. I'm determined to prove I can get my act together."

Though Zoe professed to be sober, how could he be sure she wouldn't stray back into that old lifestyle?

However, they shared something in common—he, too, had lost everything and struggled daily with trying to earn back those pieces of his soul that had been chipped away and traded until redemption seemed like an almost unachievable hope.

Chapter Three

Could she really do this?

Zoe closed her eyes, took a deep breath and squared her shoulders. Yes, she could. Time to stop questioning and start proving.

After Sully left Canine Companions, he called a couple of hours later, asking if Zoe was still interested in working with his family.

So here she was.

She released her air-filled lungs and rang the doorbell. Standing on the front porch of Caleb's tan ranch with chocolate-colored shutters, she heard the sounds of a dog barking, and a child's cry, then a man's raised voice echoed through the storm door.

Her stomach twisted. What was she getting herself into?

If she could handle four years of prison, surely she could handle a dog and a couple of kids. After all, she had a kid of her own, right?

One she wasn't currently raising…

The front door opened, jerking her out of her thoughts. Sully stood in the doorway wearing a wet T-shirt and faded jeans, barefoot. His hair looked like it had been combed with a garden rake. Lines pinched his taut jaw.

Apparently not a good morning at the Sullivan household.

She swallowed the tangle of nerves twining around her windpipe and smiled. "Good morning."

"That's debatable. Come on in."

She wouldn't let his growl diffuse her enthusiasm, but she didn't want to intrude, either. "If this is a bad time, I can come back later."

Sully breathed deeply, then ran his hands through his hair. "No time like the present. Just don't expect miracles."

She stepped through the screen door he opened for her, then pulled her lips between her teeth to bite back the laugh gurgling in her throat.

Sully's two daughters stood about four feet behind him, wearing oversize T-shirts. Their wet hair soaked the cotton fabric as puddles formed on the ceramic tile around their feet.

Riley barked from somewhere deeper in the house, then raced down the hall with something in his mouth. He rushed over to Sully, dropped it at his master's feet, barked, then waited for expected praise over his trophy.

Sully scooped the toy off the floor, stared at it, then groaned. He thrust it behind his back and scrubbed his free hand over his face.

He glanced at Zoe. "We have a lot of work to do."

For some reason, she didn't think he was referring to only dog training. The man looked exhausted, and it was only nine in the morning.

They decided to schedule their appointments for mornings when the girls would be refreshed and wide-awake after breakfast. Then Sully could work for a couple of hours while they napped. Seemed ideal on paper.

"Daddy, are you holding Melly Moon?"

Sully's shoulders sagged. Looking at his oldest daughter, he held out a headless doll. "I'm sorry, Ella. Riley found Melly Moon."

Ella snatched the doll from him and crushed it to her chest. Tears filled her eyes and spilled over her rounded cheeks. "No, Daddy. Not my Melly."

"I'm sorry, sweetheart. Maybe we can fix it."

"But she won't be the same."

Caleb Sullivan, the person she admired so much in college, who used to lock up criminals and preserve justice, looked about wiped out after a few hours with two young girls and a frisky pup.

Riley bounded back into the room and dropped something at Zoe's feet. She picked it up to find an orange-haired chubby face adorned with glittery stars and moons smiling at her. The newly decapitated Melly Moon.

At that moment, Ella glanced at Zoe, then let out a wail. She jumped into Sully's arms and buried her face in his chest, sobbing as if her heart were broken.

His other daughter stood rooted to the spot with a fearful look on her face.

The pitiful sight tugged at Zoe's heart.

She examined the doll head and realized it was made of cloth. Riley had ripped it off at the seam. She dug through her purse to find her travel-size sewing kit, then stepped closer to Sully and Ella. Sitting cross-legged on the floor next to him, her knee brushed his, but she didn't move, savoring the very brief contact.

She touched the sobbing child's shoulder, then carefully slid the girl's tangled hair behind her ear. "Ella, I can fix Melly Moon."

Sniffling, Ella peeked out from behind Sully's shoulder. "But it won't be the same."

"No, maybe not exactly the same, but I think you'll still love Melly anyway, won't you?"

She nodded.

Zoe held out her hand. "May I see Melly Moon?"

Ella tightened her grip on the headless doll and shook her head.

Sully shuffled his position and winced. "Let's move into the living room."

Still holding Ella, he reached for Ava's hand. Zoe followed them into the living room and sat on the end of the leather couch opposite from Sully.

He lifted the hem of the oversize T-shirt Ella wore and wiped the traces of tears from her face. "Hey, Ella, remember when Ava cut her finger?"

Ella nodded again. "There was a lot of blood, and she cried."

"Yes, she did. It hurt a lot." Caleb reached for Ava and pulled her gently to him. He opened his youngest daughter's hand and rubbed his thumb across the tiny knuckles on her pointer finger. "The doctor put two small stitches in it. Her finger isn't the way it was before because now it has a tiny scar, but her finger still works just as well. If Zoe sews Melly Moon's head back on, you may be able to see where she stitched, but Melly Moon will be in one piece and almost as good as new."

Ella considered that a moment, then handed the doll over to Zoe. She plopped onto Sully's leg to watch.

Sully's face twisted in pain as he readjusted both girls on his lap.

The man needed a shower, strong coffee and a nap… not necessarily in that order.

Zoe threaded her needle. With three pairs of expectant eyes watching her, she felt more nervous about this than training Riley. Dogs were her superpower. Sewing, on the other hand…

With small, even stitches, she secured Melly's head to her body, knotted the thread, then bit off the excess. She gave the head a gentle tug. Pleased with its strength, she handed the doll to Ella. "Here you go, sweetie."

Ella took the doll and inspected its neck. "I can't see where you sewed."

That was the point.

Sully nudged his daughter. "What do you say to Miss Zoe?"

Ella flew off Sully's lap and flung her arms around Zoe's neck, taking her by surprise. "Thank you, Miss Zoe. You saved Melly Moon. You're the best."

The girl's words pricked the fragile shell around Zoe's heart. It had been a long time since anyone had considered her the best at anything. The warmth of the little girl's body pressing against Zoe's chest seeped into her soul, fanning the flicker of a spark she thought had been snuffed out long ago.

Hope.

Careful not to poke the child with her needle, Zoe wrapped her arms around Ella and hugged her close. "You're welcome, sweetie."

Ella pulled away from Zoe and hugged Melly while she twirled through the living room. "Look, Avie, isn't Miss Zoe the best?"

Ava cast a shy glance in Zoe's direction and gave her a small smile. Then she nodded.

Did Sully realize how blessed he was to have such sweet daughters?

The look of love he wore answered her question. He would never stop loving his daughters, no matter what they did.

A pang pinched her heart. She wasn't going there.

Eyes up and feet forward. Her new mantra.

Sully pushed to his feet, not quite swallowing a groan, then held out a hand to her. She took it and stood, not wanting to release his warm, strong grip.

He gave her fingers a gentle squeeze before releasing them. "You're amazing. Thank you."

"No problem."

"What a morning."

"What happened?" Zoe returned the needle and thread to its case, then stowed everything back in her purse.

"What didn't happen would be quicker to answer. Ava woke up with a wet bed. I was trying to give them a bath and keep Riley out of their room when you arrived. I'm sorry you walked into chaos."

She placed a hand on his upper arm. "Sully, relax. It's just fine."

"Thanks. That's cool of you to say. It means a lot. Let me get the girls some breakfast, then we can talk about training the monster if you're still up to it."

"I'm game if you are."

"Yeah, after this morning, we need to do something fast." He gathered a bundle of unfolded laundry off the couch and righted a beige throw pillow. "Have a seat and I'll get them squared away. Then we can talk about how to proceed."

"What can I do to help?"

"Nothing. I'll take care of it."

Zoe reached for his arm and tried not to think about the strength radiating from his muscular form. "Sully, stop being stubborn. You're a great dad. But asking for help isn't a sign of weakness, you know."

Sully stared at her for a long moment, then sighed. Instead of answering, he sat on the couch cushion, dropped the laundry at his feet and wrapped his hands around his head. "How do single parents do this, Zoe? How did you handle it with Griffin?" Then, as if realizing what he had just said, crimson rose above the collar of his shirt and colored his neck. "Sorry, I mean, before…"

"Listen, Sully, I'm the last person qualified to give you parenting advice. I'm probably the world's worst mom, but I'm so thankful for my parents and my brother, Ian. They deserve all the credit for Griffin being such a great kid. But, the way I see it, you're trying too hard to prove you're some kind of superdad."

"I'm all they have."

"Doesn't mean you have to be perfect. Let's face it, we all need help every now and then. The way you handled Melly Moon was great. You proved to be a hero to your daughter."

"You were the one who saved the day with your mad sewing skills."

"My point is you're doing what matters. Focus on the big stuff. Who cares about a wet bed? Sheets can be washed. Give the girls what they need most—your unconditional love."

"That's a given. Thanks, Zoe. There's coffee in the kitchen. Help yourself to some. I need to get the girls dressed."

They headed in different directions—Sully followed Ella's giggles down the hall while Zoe went to the kitchen.

She searched the cupboards for two mugs and filled them with coffee. She pulled out three bowls and set them on the round table under the window. She found two boxes of cereal and grabbed milk and apple juice from the fridge. Cups, napkins and spoons completed the table settings.

Once Sully and the girls had some breakfast and were a little more relaxed after this morning's calamity, then they could focus on working out the best training plan for Riley.

Excitement brewed, but she couldn't quite determine if it was for finally using her dog-training skills or for the amount of time she'd be spending with Sully and the girls.

She'd have to work hard to keep an emotional distance. After all, she couldn't risk her heart over something that could never be.

She couldn't mix business and pleasure, especially with this family. Sully deserved someone who could give him a shining future, not one with a clouded past.

How could two little girls make such a mess?

He needed to do better at keeping things together.

Caleb stepped over stuffed animals, a coloring book and several scattered crayons to grab Ava's wet pajamas off the girls' bedroom floor.

After they'd moved to Shelby Lake, Caleb had called his sister, Sarah, for help in setting up the girls' bedroom. He didn't even want to think about his credit card bill next month.

Sarah had selected white twin beds with matching

purple-and-green comforters and curtains. Flower-shaped throw rugs lay in front of matching white dressers with mirrors.

Apparently she felt the girls needed every stuffed animal the toy store had in stock. Not to mention the dollhouse in the corner of the room. A basket of books sat between two fairy-princess beanbag chairs under the window.

A new room for a fresh start.

Giggling in the bathroom pulled him out of his thoughts. He dropped the wet clothes on the pile of dirty towels in the girls' hamper in the closet, and then strode down the hall.

Within two minutes, he had both girls dressed, hair brushed in some semblance of order and shooed them out of the room so he could empty the tub.

Once the bathroom looked less like a wrecking zone, he headed for the kitchen. He found the girls huddled together on the couch in the living room with Ella aiming the remote at the TV as she sang along with Dora the Explorer in Spanish.

Caleb reached for the remote and flicked off the cartoon. He held out his hands to them. "Come on, girls. Let's find you some breakfast."

He didn't realize how much he had missed the little touches of domesticity until he walked into the kitchen holding the girls' hands and found the table already set.

That was one thing he never took for granted while he was married. He always made sure he let Val know how much he appreciated what she did for him.

"You didn't have to do this." He looked at Zoe, leaning against the kitchen counter, coffee mug in one hand and the newspaper folded open in the other.

She smiled at him over the edge of her mug. "I wanted to. You had your hands full, and I figured I could be a little useful. Hope you don't mind that I went through your cupboards."

He waved away her concern. "Doesn't bother me one bit." In fact, it warmed him a little to think she was comfortable enough with him and his home to do that. But she wasn't here to be their housekeeper.

No, in fact, he needed to get a better handle on this parenting thing because he was determined to give his daughters the stability they needed.

He buckled the girls into their booster seats and motioned for Zoe to sit in one of the empty chairs. Once she did, he sat across from her and folded his hands. "Girls, let's say our prayers before we eat."

They bowed their heads, and Caleb gave thanks for the food. Under his breath, he thanked God for reconnecting him with Zoe again. He didn't know what God's plan was for the two of them, but he didn't believe seeing her again was a coincidence. He'd go with it until God steered him in a different direction.

Caleb poured cereal and milk into the girls' bowls. He pushed his bowl out of the way and reached for his coffee mug. After the first couple of sips, he started to feel almost human again. Almost.

Caleb leaned forward and rested his elbows on the table.

Ella tapped his arm with her spoon. "Daddy, no elbows on the table."

"You're right, sweetie. I forgot." Caleb smiled at her as he pulled his elbows down and rested his forearms on the table.

"It's okay. Everybody makes mistakes."

And he'd made more than his fair share of them. He smoothed a hand over Ella's drying hair and shifted his attention to Zoe.

She watched them with a mix of sadness and wistfulness. What was she thinking?

Even in the short time they've been reacquainted, Caleb could see she wasn't the same girl he'd known at school. The woman sitting across from him carried heavy burdens. Her eyes used to sparkle with laughter and a touch of mischief. Now they had been dulled with pain and brokenness.

He wanted to see her filled with joy once again, not return to a past life they'd once shared. No, those days were over. But perhaps this could be a new season of fresh starts for both of them.

She reached for Ava's napkin and wiped the milk dripping off her chin. "I can stay for another hour if you'd like to get a start on Riley's training."

He glanced at his watch to see their designated hour was almost up. She was right—the morning hadn't gone as expected. "Yes, that would be great. But only if you're sure."

She smiled. "It's not a problem as long as I'm not messing up your plans." At the shake of his head, she continued, "I'd like you to have some basics in place before I leave. Let me just grab my bag so we can go over paperwork and a couple different training plans." She pushed back her chair and stood. "Mind if we talk in the living room? That way I can see how the girls interact with Riley and his reactions to his surroundings."

"No, that's just fine."

As she walked past him to retrieve her bag, he caught a whiff of her perfume, a sweet fragrance that reawakened emotions he thought were forever locked behind a door marked Do Not Enter.

Maybe not.

Ella drained her juice and wiped her mouth with her napkin. "Daddy, may I get down? I'm all done."

He glanced at Ava. "Are you ready to get down, too, Aves?"

She nodded and smiled, but didn't say a word.

She'd talk. In her time.

He slid out their chairs and helped them down. "Let's go into the living room so Daddy can talk to Miss Zoe, okay?"

They headed for the living room to find that Zoe had laid a couple of folders on the coffee table and sat back against the cushion to wait for them. Her long fingers stroked Riley's fur as he curled in her lap.

As he settled beside her and flung an arm over the back of the couch, Riley stirred. His ears perked. He bounded off Zoe's lap and jumped on Caleb's chest.

Caleb turned his face away from Riley's rough tongue and moved the pup into a better position on his lap.

Zoe reached for the folders and handed one to him. "I'm sure Leona gave you some of this material already when you met with her, but I included it in the packet so it would be together in one place. I'm kind of OCD like that."

"No worries. Despite the chaos you walked into this morning, I'm an organized person, too."

"No wonder we get along well." The smile that spread across her face warmed his insides faster than the coffee he'd downed a few minutes ago.

Zoe reviewed the papers in the packet—Leona's advertising brochure for dog-training options, a more detailed letter explaining policies and practices, and then an in-home behavior-training program. "At any time, if you're dissatisfied with Riley's progress or my training, contact Leona and she will refund your money. All of her programs offer a money-back guarantee. Any questions?"

"Would it be possible to do trainings several times a week instead of spreading them out over the next six or eight weeks?"

"I'm sure we can work something out. Once you sign the release form, we can get started this morning with some basics."

Caleb leaned forward, upsetting Riley's comfortable sleeping spot. Once the dog bounced off his lap, Caleb reached for the Canine Companions pen and scribbled his signature where Zoe had marked an X. Just knowing they were heading in the right direction helped him to lean into hope—something he hadn't done in a while.

"The key to Riley's training is going to be consistency. Training a puppy is similar to caring for your daughters—you want to stay positive, remain patient and praise him for doing well. When you came into Canine Companions, you seemed frustrated."

That was an understatement.

Caleb rubbed a hand over his jaw. "I guess you could say that."

"Don't worry. By the time we're finished, Riley will be the best-behaved pup in town."

With the girls in tow and Riley nipping at his heels, he gave Zoe a tour of the house and backyard. She suggested he move Riley's crate into his bedroom to give the little guy some extra security.

Out in the yard, the morning temperatures were climbing already. As the girls chased each other, Zoe showed him how to take the lead when they snapped the leash onto Riley.

Back in the house, she demonstrated how to stay consistent with crate training. She helped Ella and Ava give Riley a treat. Each time Riley did as instructed, she praised him with words and affectionate touches, then offered him a small treat.

By the time their hour was up, Caleb felt more confident about the pup not destroying everything in the house. But he was reluctant to walk Zoe to the door.

She handed him a piece of paper. "Here's a list of things that will help you with training. If you give Riley toys to chew on, he'll leave your personal belongings alone. Try to remember he's like a toddler and needs gentle guidance and instruction to help learn positive behaviors."

He glanced at the sheet, then looked at her. "You're a natural at this, Zoe."

She dropped her gaze to her feet and tucked a loose strand of hair behind her ear. "I love animals, especially dogs. Always have. They're forgiving and eager to please. I get them, and they get me."

"I can see why. Thanks, Zoe. For everything."

She placed a hand on his forearm and squeezed. "My pleasure, Sully. I'm really looking forward to this."

"Me, too." He curled his fingers over his arm where her hand had been to lock in the feel of her tender touch against his skin.

Maybe, by working together, they'd have an opportunity to revive the past connection they'd once shared. Maybe he could be the one to fill her eyes with joy once again. Would she give a broken has-been like him a chance?

He'd let things move at a natural pace. He wouldn't rush her into anything she didn't want, but he wasn't about to lose her friendship again.

Chapter Four

With the sunshine warming her face and Harper by her side as they walked to Ian and Agnes's house, Zoe refused to let anything spoil the rest of her day.

She guided Harper up the front steps to the cottage Ian had bought for his wife, Agnes, a little over a year ago as a wedding gift. Best friends for more than twenty years, the two of them had finally wised up to what everyone else had known for a long time—they belonged together.

Now they had everything they'd always wanted.

Would she ever find *her* dreams?

Ones that didn't include Sully or his adorable daughters?

After she'd left his place, she had returned to Canine Companions. Leona approved her training arrangements with him and filed his paperwork. She did take a minute to caution Zoe about maintaining a professional distance. Zoe assured her she had nothing to worry about. Sully had his hands full with his daughters right now. The last thing he needed was a relationship with a convicted felon.

A shout sounded from behind the cottage. Zoe led Harper to the fenced-in backyard overlooking the lake.

Gray smoke plumed from the grill on the edge of the patio while the scent of barbecue drifted with the afternoon breeze. A picnic table had been covered with a blue gingham tablecloth while a canning jar filled with wildflowers anchored it down.

The one who attracted her attention was the nine-year-old boy dressed in an Iron Man T-shirt and black basketball shorts, with scruffy golden-brown hair that looked like it needed to be cut and green eyes with gold flecks like her own.

Her son, Griffin—the only decent thing she'd ever done in her life.

But she'd failed him, too.

Mom, Agnes and Griffin stood off to the side while Ian hefted a horseshoe in his hand, then pitched it. Metal clanked against metal as the shoe rung around the stake. He leaned back and let out a shout of joy, then high-fived Dad.

Dad walked to the opposite stake and gathered their horseshoes, then stepped off to the side while Mom, Agnes and Griffin lined up to throw their shoes.

Why did she always feel like an unwanted guest at her own family dinners?

Probably because she hadn't felt like a family member in such a long time. Sometimes the James family expectations had her retreating inside her shell, wanting to be more of a guest than an actual participant. That way, her parents' disappointment in her actions wouldn't hurt so much.

Dad glanced up and saw Zoe standing by the gate. He nodded at her, then whispered in Mom's ear. Mom turned and smiled, then beckoned her into the fence. "Zoe, come join us."

Spying her, Griffin raced for the gate. He flung it open and hurled himself against her waist. "Mom! You made it."

Zoe wrapped her arms around him. "Of course. How could I resist Aunt Agnes's barbecue and dinner with my favorite guy?"

Griffin released her and smiled wide, showing a small gap between his top front teeth. He was growing too quickly, and she was missing most of it.

"So I come in second after the barbecue?"

"Priorities, dude. Priorities." She ruffled his hair and made a mental note to call for an appointment to get it chopped before school started next week.

"Yeah, whatever. Wanna throw some shoes with us? You can be on Grandpa's team."

Dad would love that.

Harper barked and circled around Griffin's legs. He dropped to the ground and buried his face in the dog's black coat. "Hey, girl."

He released Harper's harness to allow her to run in the yard and handed it to Zoe. She wrapped the leash and harness and dropped them in the bag that held Harper's food and dishes. She followed Griffin back to the horseshoe pit.

She hugged Mom and Agnes, then waved to Dad and Ian.

"How was work, honey?" Mom slid an arm around her waist.

"Good, Mom. Thanks."

Agnes glanced at her watch, then handed her horseshoes to Zoe. "Throw for me. I need to get dinner on the table. I hope y'all are hungry. We have ribs and all the fixin's."

"Sounds great."

Dad stood behind Griffin and covered his grandson's small hand with his larger one. Together they swung their arms a couple of times to gauge the rhythm of the motion. Then Dad stepped back and nodded to Griffin.

Griff scrunched up his eyebrows and bit the corner of his lip as he stepped forward and focused on the opposite stake. He swung his arm back, then pitched the horseshoe.

It clanked around the iron stake, then thumped to the ground.

Griffin thrust both fists in the air. "Yeah!" He turned to her. "Did you see that, Mom? I did it."

"You sure did, but then I had no doubt you could do it."

Dad gathered the horseshoes, then ambled over to Griffin. "Way to go, bubba. You scored the winning point."

"Yes!" He punched the air over his head a few more times to celebrate his victory.

A whistle pierced the air. Agnes stood on the patio and waved everyone toward her. "Time to eat. Let's wash up, y'all."

Griffin jumped to his feet and patted his thigh. "Let's go, Harper."

Harper barked in agreement, then raced Griffin to the house.

Once everyone had washed up, they formed a circle on the patio and grabbed hands for prayer. Zoe found herself between Griffin and Dad. As she held on to her son's hand, which was almost as big as her own, she placed hers in Dad's.

His warm, calloused fingers closed around hers. For

a moment, she pretended all was right in the world, and she was Daddy's little girl once again.

How many times had he reached out a hand to help her when she had fallen? How many times had he caressed her hair with those hands? How many times had he taught her how to do something, like he did with Griffin?

She missed his terms of endearment, the closeness they once shared. When she was released from prison, Dad claimed to have forgiven her—he'd even worked hard to help Mom and Ian get Agape House opened when a series of setbacks had threatened it. But did he truly forgive her—in his heart where it mattered most?

She'd hurt him deeply, and it would take time for those wounds to heal. She couldn't erase the past, but she'd do her best not to repeat it. She'd earn back his pride and prove that she was worthy of loving.

And maybe that started with accepting Sully's offer to help his daughters learn how to manage their new dog.

As soon as Ian concluded the prayer, Dad gave her hand a gentle squeeze, then released it.

"Wake up, Mom." Griffin jerked on her arm, pulling her from her thoughts.

"Sorry, honey. Just deep in thought."

"Yeah, I saw. How about getting deep in those ribs on the table?"

"Sounds good to me. Lead the way."

She followed Griffin and sat at the opposite end of the picnic table from Dad. She glanced down the table to find him watching her, but the moment she caught his eye, he looked away. Folding her hands in her lap, she stared at the pattern on the tablecloth.

Nudging her, Ian handed her a paper plate. "You okay?"

She looked at him and smiled. "Yes, fine."

He passed a platter piled with steaming, golden ears of corn. She grabbed the tongs and dropped an ear on her plate, then passed it across the table to Mom.

At her feet, Harper stirred. Her eyes perked as tires crunched in the front driveway. She barked and trotted for the front of the house.

"Expecting someone to join us, Ian?" Mom asked from across the table.

"Nope. Everyone's here." Ian stood and moved away from the table. "I'll be right back."

He followed Harper around the side of the house. Zoe buttered her corn and was about to take bite when Ian returned to the backyard.

But he wasn't alone.

A police officer carrying a manila envelope followed him.

Dad shot a glance at her and frowned.

Zoe heaved a sigh and shook her head. Of course, if the police were involved, it had to have something to do with her. She dropped her corn on her plate and folded her arms on the table.

Ian's lips thinned as he approached the picnic table. He exchanged glances with Agnes.

Agnes jumped up from the table. "Hey, Griffin. Wanna help me with the apple pie in the kitchen?"

Butter smeared Griffin's lips. "But we just started eating."

She smiled and nodded toward the house. "Let's bring it out anyway. We can have it with our ribs and corn."

"Works for me." He wiped his mouth with his hand and hopped up from his seat.

Once the door to the house closed behind them, Dad pushed to his feet. "What's going on, Ian?"

Ian jerked a thumb at the cop. "Officer Reynolds has something for you and Mom."

"Us? How'd you know we were here?" Mom wiped her mouth with a napkin and left the table to stand next to Dad.

Officer Reynolds removed his sunglasses and hooked them on the breast pocket of his dark blue uniform. He crossed his hands in front of him. "I stopped by your house, but no one was there. Your neighbor—a Mrs. Kingsley—was in the yard and told me where I could find you."

Agnes's mom.

Dad folded his arms over his chest. "What can I do for you, Officer?"

"Sir, I've been directed to give you this." He handed Dad the envelope.

Dad tore it open and scanned the contents. His gaze bounced off her and landed on Mom. Dad scrubbed a hand over his face. He crumpled the papers in his white-knuckled grip. "Are you serious?"

The officer held up his hands. "I was instructed to deliver the envelope. I'm unaware of the contents."

"Right. Thank you." Dad extended his hand to the officer.

The officer shook Dad's hand, nodded to Mom, then turned to head back to the driveway.

Mom pressed her hand on Dad's arm, a frown creasing her forehead. "What's going on, Pete?"

Dad released his hold on the papers and tossed them on the table. "It's a petition for custody of Griffin."

"Griffin? Why, that's ridiculous. By whom?" Mom

picked up the papers, scanned them and then sucked in a breath. Her eyes darted to Zoe as her voice dropped to a whisper. "Davis and Marcia Jacoby."

Zoe jumped up from her seat and snatched the papers out of her mom's hands. As she scanned the legalese, her heart leaped to her throat.

This couldn't be happening.

She forced back the acid burning her throat and searched Dad's face for reassurance. "They can't do that, can they?"

"I'm afraid they can." Dad leaned against the table and wrapped an arm around Mom's shoulders, drawing her to his side. "Doesn't mean they'll win. We'll make sure of that."

She hoped so.

Griffin had thrived in her parents' custody while her morale wasted away behind bars.

He deserved so much more.

Because of the choices she'd made, their lives were drastically different than from the day she looked in his newborn eyes and promised she'd be the best mom she could.

She wanted to be the kind of mom who baked cookies and helped with classroom parties and served on the PTA. She'd been working hard to prove she could be the one who regained custody of her son, rather than grandparents who would do anything in their power to destroy her.

Was Zoe crazy to imagine their walk in the park wasn't a training session but a family outing?

As Sully held on to the leash, Riley trotted at his side. Giggling, Ella and Ava ran ahead of them on the path that trailed along the river, their ponytails bouncing against the backs of their matching pink tank tops. They chased Griffin, who jogged ahead but kept looking over his shoulder to see how close they were.

Yes, definitely crazy.

And, for one thing, she was getting way ahead of herself. The last thing she needed was to confuse the boundaries between personal and professional. That wasn't what Sully signed up for. Besides, he had his hands full with the girls and his job. And she didn't need some guy to rescue her.

But Sully wasn't some guy...

For a moment, though, she could pretend. Just for a moment she could pretend he was her husband, and the girls were hers, along with Griffin, of course.

In addition to being a dog trainer, she'd have a husband, a family. She'd belong. Without the baggage of her past holding her back.

When she'd arrived at Caleb's for their session and suggested the park, he was all for it, even with Griffin and Harper joining them. And the girls loved the idea. After a week of training at their house, she figured Riley could handle the distractions in the park.

The morning sunshine cast a glow across the Shelby Lake River, bleaching the water and making it shimmer like polished silver.

A family of ducks swam to the bank and waddled to the grass, catching the girls' attention. They hurried after them, causing the ducks to squawk and flap their wings.

"Girls, stay on the path, away from the bank."

"Okay, Daddy." Ella half turned and waved. She reached for Ava's hand and pulled her back onto the gravel path winding along the riverbank.

Riley barked and tugged on his leash. Sully tightened his hold. "Riley, quiet."

Riley looked at Sully, then back at the ducks, but he obeyed.

Sully stooped and petted his head. "Good boy." He fished a small treat out of his pocket, commanded Riley to sit and then fed it to him. His dark blue Henley-style shirt stretched across his back.

Zoe hesitated, then placed a hand on Sully's shoulder. "You handled that well." She pulled her hand away before she did something stupid like run it across the sun-warmed fabric and into his hair.

He pushed to his feet and smiled at her. "Coming to the park was a good idea. Thanks for suggesting it."

"You're welcome. And thanks for letting Griffin and Harper tag along."

"Hey, no problem. Your son seems like a great kid."

"He's the best. I figured the park offered many distractions, so it's a great way to get Riley acclimated to new environments and follow commands outside of his comfort zone."

The distractions for Riley were nothing compared to the ones she felt walking next to Sully. The scent of his soap lingered on his skin. The morning breeze ruffled his hair.

He bumped her shoulder with his. "You're really good at your job."

His praise warmed her faster than the rays of sunshine. Like Riley, she was eager to prove she could do this. "Thanks. I enjoy what I do."

"Your passion shows. Must make your job feel less like work."

"I'm blessed to be working for Leona. Canine Companions allows me to spend a lot of time with my favorite animals." They followed the path past the picnic pavilion until the playground came into view.

Two little boys chased each other around the merry-go-round. A young woman pushed a toddler on the swings. A man stood at the bottom of the slide promising to catch a boy sitting at the top with a scared expression on his face.

Zoe tucked her hair behind her ear and shifted her gaze to Sully. "What about you? How do you want to spend the rest of your life?"

Sully sighed and tugged his fingers through his hair. "All I've ever wanted was to be a cop. With this new job, I can retain my shield and help kids know they are enough without descending into drugs and alcohol abuse."

"Sounds like you're the right guy for the job."

"Thanks. It's not what I'm used to, so it will be an adjustment."

With Ava at her heels, Ella skipped over to them and tugged on Sully's arm. "Daddy, Avie and I want to play in the sandbox, don't we, Avie?"

Ava nodded.

Sully glanced at Zoe. "Do you mind?"

"No, of course not."

"Okay, go ahead, girls." He pointed to a bench. "Zoe and I will sit right there and watch you."

They settled on the warm metal as the girls ran hand in hand to the sandbox.

"Here, Mom." Griffin handed over Harper's leash, then sat between the girls in the sandbox. He helped dig up mounds of sand for them to mold and shape. He'd make a great big brother someday.

Once Harper curled up in the shade of the bench, Zoe

shifted so she wouldn't be brushing against Sully. Did he sit that close to her on purpose? "Your daughters seem to be adjusting well."

"For the most part, I think they are. We still have moments, especially when they're tired." He gazed at the girls as they patted sand into a mound. The tender expression he wore every time he talked about the girls caused Zoe to yearn for the days when her own dad looked at her like that.

"That's normal with any kid. You're a great dad, Sully." He was close enough for her to see the two-inch scar on his jaw under his morning shadow.

He smiled, the lines deepening around his eyes. "I'm trying. It's a challenge at times, especially when Ella asks when her mommy is coming back."

"I'm sorry. That must be so hard. Can I ask you a personal question?"

"Shoot."

"Why doesn't Ava speak?"

Sully leaned back and rested his elbows on the top of the bench. To the passerby, he appeared relaxed, but the tic in his jaw and his clenched hands told a different story.

"Sweet little Ava used to chatter constantly, but after my injury and Val walking out on us, she clammed up and hasn't spoken since. My sister wants me to make an appointment with an early-intervention specialist. She's had a lot of changes recently. When I saw her with Riley and Harper that day in the park, I figured adopting a dog would help her to relax again and start speaking."

"She may. Give it time."

Ella stepped out of the sandbox and ran barefoot over to their bench. Sand coated her legs and denim shorts. "Daddy, Avie and I are thirsty."

"Your drinks are in the car." Sully pushed to his feet.

Zoe pressed a hand on his arm. "You stay here. I can get them for you."

He fished his keys out of the front pocket of his cargo shorts and handed them to her. "There's a small red cooler in the trunk with water bottles in it."

"I'll be back in a minute." She jogged across the grass to the parking lot where Sully's black sedan was parked in the shade. She found the soft-sided cooler and slung the strap over her shoulder before slamming the trunk closed and returning back to the playground.

Her steps slowed as she cut across the grass. Sully stood talking to a woman dressed in a light blue fitted tank top and black workout capris. A white sport visor and sunglasses shaded the woman's face. She had an arm around Griffin's shoulders and held him close to her side.

Who was she, and how did she know her son? A teacher? Someone from church?

As she turned, though, Zoe caught a better look at her profile. She sucked in a breath and took a few steps back as her heart hammered against her ribs. Her gaze darted between the sandbox where the girls continued to play and Sully's car. There wasn't any place for her to go without drawing attention. And that was the last thing she wanted at this moment.

Maybe she could duck around the small cement building that housed the park's public restrooms.

Yes, that's what she'd do—retreat inside until the woman was gone. She didn't care if it made her look cowardly. Better a coward than getting in a confrontation in front of Sully and his daughters. And Griffin.

She walked backward a few steps. About ten more and she could slip inside unnoticed.

Riley had been resting in the cool shade under the bench. He lifted his head, spied Zoe and barked, drawing everyone's attention to her.

Her feet froze.

She tried to silence him with hand signals, but the little pup jumped up and raced toward her, only to be stopped by Sully's grip on the dog's leash.

Could she still rush inside without looking completely ridiculous?

Sully looked at the woman, then at Zoe with an expression she couldn't quite decipher. It was similar to the one he wore when he opened the door on their first day of training—a cross between fatigue and surrender.

Continuing to bark at Zoe, Riley ran around and through Sully's legs, entangling him with the leash.

Ella jumped up from the sandbox and skipped over to her. "Miss Zoe, can I have a drink, please?"

So much for anonymity.

The woman's head shot up. She removed her sunglasses, then seared Zoe with a narrowed-eyed glare. Her lips thinned as she tightened her grip on Griffin's shoulders. "Zoe. A friend of yours, Caleb?"

He rubbed a hand over his face and sighed. "Yes, Mrs. Jacoby, she is."

"You'd do well to choose better friends. You, of all people, should know better than to be consorting with someone like her."

"Zoe's changed."

"People like her never change." Mrs. Jacoby's nostrils flared. "Be careful, Caleb. You don't want your…friend to cause problems between you and your family."

"Are you threatening me?"

"Not at all—more like a friendly word of caution."

Griffin shrugged Mrs. Jacoby's hand off his shoulder and whirled around, scowling. "Hey, don't talk about my mom like that."

He ran to Zoe. She pulled him against her and wrapped her arms over his chest.

"Enjoy him while you have the chance," Mrs. Jacoby slid her sunglasses back on her face and smoothed down the front of her shirt.

Ice frosted Zoe's veins as the woman's unspoken threat lingered between them, taunting her. The Jacobys had a lot of money and lawyers, but Zoe prayed God would go to battle on her behalf. She couldn't lose her son, especially to grandparents who would poison him against her.

Sully studied her, but she refused to wither. He returned his attention to Mrs. Jacoby. "If you'll excuse us, I need to get the girls home."

Without waiting for a response, he spun around and lifted Ava out of the sandbox. He brushed sand off her denim shorts, then hoisted her on his hip. Her hands slid around his neck as he turned around and held out a hand to his oldest daughter. "Come on, Ells. Let's go home."

"But Daddy—" Ella scrunched up her face and stomped her foot.

He dropped to his haunches, then grimaced. He rubbed his right thigh. "Sweetie, we can come back later."

"Why can't we just stay now?" Her bottom lip popped out in a pout.

"We came to help Riley get used to the park, remember? Our time with Miss Zoe and Griffin is almost up. We'll come back later, and you can play longer."

"Promise?"

"I can't promise because I don't know what may come up, but I do know Aunt Sarah is coming over today, so maybe we can come back before dinner. How does that sound?"

"Yay! Aunt Sarah!" She launched herself into his arms and hugged him.

He hooked their sandals over his fingers, then held each of their hands and walked them across the stretch of grass to the car. Sully tossed their shoes on the floor of the car as they climbed into their car seats. After buckling them and handing them bottles of water, he closed the door and sighed.

Zoe held out Harper's leash to Griffin. "Hey, Griff, how about if you take Harper to the car? I need to talk to Sully for a minute."

"Okay, Mom." Griffin looked at Sully a moment, then took Harper's leash and patted the side of his leg. "Come on, Harper. Let's go."

As he ran with Harper to the car, Sully braced a hand against the door frame and faced Zoe with his other hand on his hip. "What's up?"

She fingered her necklace. "I'm sorry for what happened back there, and being the reason the girls have to leave. They were having a good time."

He glanced at his watch. "No, it's a good time to leave. Our hour is almost up. I'll take the girls home and keep them busy until lunch. My sister is coming by this afternoon to watch them while I go into work for a few hours."

Zoe kicked at the pavement with the toe of her sandal. "Listen, Sully, maybe Mrs. Jacoby is right. I'll talk to Leona and find another trainer for you. You don't need someone like me around the girls."

"Someone like you?" He muttered something under his breath, then tipped up her chin so she'd meet his eyes.

Lines bracketed his thinned lips. "Why are you even listening to her?"

She wanted to look away so he couldn't see the shame in her eyes, but his hand kept a gentle but firm hold on her face. She reached up and pulled his hand away, but didn't let it go. For a moment she needed the strength his touch offered. "She hates me. I killed her son."

He reached out and tucked a loose piece of hair behind her ear and lowered his voice. "Zoe, what happened was tragic. There's no denying that. And you'll carry that with you for the rest of your life. I can't even imagine what you're dealing with, but you're not that same woman. You've paid the price for what happened."

She glanced at the backseat where the girls rested their heads against their car seats, half-asleep. "But what about the girls?"

"What about them? You've shown them nothing but love and respect. They adore you."

She took a step back. Being so close to him was dangerous. "I'm sorry my personal life got dragged into our professional relationship."

"I chose you, Zoe, because I remember the good times we shared. I know what kind of person you are."

"I'm not that girl anymore."

"No, you're not, but I like the woman you've become. I know you're facing tough days, Zoe, but you're not alone."

She risked crossing that line between personal and professional, but she needed a friend, especially someone like Sully, who understood and could shed some legal light on her situation. "The Jacobys filed a petition for custody for Griffin. Mom and Dad's lawyers feel they have no legal grounds, especially since they've had very little to do with him since Kyle's death."

He scowled. "Surely they know that. So why are they doing it?"

"To get back at me." Zoe leaned against his car and crossed her arms over her chest. "They said since I took their son, they're doing everything in their power to take mine."

"I'm so sorry, Zoe." He cupped her face and caressed her cheek with his thumb.

"They will never forgive me for what happened to Kyle. Unfortunately, they're hurting my son in their revenge against me." The weight of the Jacobys' threats ate at her like a cancer. She rubbed her stomach, trying to massage away the ache that seemed to be a constant. "The poor kid's gone through enough. He doesn't need to be subjected to them, too."

"What can I do to help?" He curled a loose strand of hair around his finger.

She'd done what she vowed not to do—she tangled professionalism with personal. Stepping away from his car and his tender touch, she forced her lips into a smile. "Nothing, Sully. This isn't your problem."

He reached for her hand. "You're my friend. I hate seeing you in pain. I want to help you."

"There's nothing you can do. My family and I will get this sorted out. My parents have been on the phone with their attorney." She pulled her phone out of her back pocket and checked the time. "You guys did great today. I need to get going."

She tried to pull her hand out of his warm grasp, but he kept a firm hold and tugged her to him. Without a word, he enveloped her against his chest. "I'm here if you need to talk or anything."

This definitely crossed those professional boundaries, but for the moment she didn't care. Since Sully had come back into her life, he'd given her the one thing she'd been craving for a long time—friendship. The problem was, though, the more time she spent with him, the more the lines between friendship and romance were becoming blurred.

She wasn't so sure she wanted them to come back into focus.

Chapter Five

Caleb tugged his baseball hat lower over his brows as he hurried up the cement steps to the courthouse and opened the heavy wooden door.

If Zoe found out what he was doing, she'd be furious. But he needed to know…for his own peace of mind. Maybe, just maybe, he could do something to help her.

Seeing her this morning left him feeling helpless. And he hated that.

He stepped inside the building located in the center of Shelby Lake's historical district. The cool air was a welcome relief from the afternoon humidity.

Twin polished wooden staircases with nicked, curved banisters flanked walls painted the color of old parchment. Portraits of judges past and present hung on the walls and stared solemnly as he crossed the gleaming tile floor to the prothonotary's office.

He opened the frosted-glass door with the office's name etched in gold and stepped inside, closing it behind him.

The same dark wood and parchment-colored walls accented the smaller room. Framed photos of the Shelby

Lake community hanging above rows of file cabinets added sparks of color to the bland room. Two women sat behind a chest-high counter that separated visitors from their office area.

Caleb rested his arms on the counter and directed his attention to the petite brunette whose nameplate identified her as Carolyn.

She looked up from her computer and smiled. "May I help you?"

"I'd like to look at a case file."

"Criminal or civil?"

"Criminal." The word stuck in his throat like stale bread.

Carolyn pointed to the other woman, another petite brunette, talking on the phone. "Amanda's the court clerk. As soon as she's finished with her call, she'll be able to help you."

"Thanks." Caleb backed away from the counter and lowered himself into one of the metal chairs. He picked up an outdated sports magazine, leafed through it and tossed it back onto the other chair. He crossed his foot over his opposite knee and tapped his thumb against his shoe.

What was he doing here?

Why didn't he just ask Zoe?

Maybe he should leave.

He dropped his foot and started to stand when Amanda hung up the phone and stood. She motioned to Caleb. "Sorry to keep you waiting, sir. If you'll go through that side door, I'll show you how to access the public records."

If he bailed now, he'd look like an idiot for wasting the ladies' time.

He stood and opened the door that led into a file room

filled with rows of metal shelves and carousel-style filing cabinets. The room lacked the air-conditioning the outer office offered. He breathed in the scent of old paper, which took him back to studying in the campus library during his college days.

Zoe had been a work-study student at the library, and he made sure he had a lot of studying to do when he knew she'd be working. With his focus more on her than his assignments, it was a wonder he'd managed to graduate.

Amanda moved to a computer and glanced at him. "What's the case number?"

"I'm not sure. The defendant was James. Zoe James."

The woman clicked a few keys, scribbled numbers on a notepad sitting beside the computer and tore off the paper. Brushing past him, she walked through the file cabinets until she found what she was looking for. She rolled out the files, retrieved a legal-size folder and handed it to him.

She nodded toward the table where the computer sat. "You're welcome to use that table to read the case, if you'd like. The computer has internet access if you need to do more research. Once you're finished, bring the folder back to me, and I'll file it. Let me know if you need anything else."

"Thanks."

As she returned to her desk, Caleb pulled out a straight-backed wooden chair and sat, staring at the folder he'd dropped on the table.

Overhead, the fluorescent lights hummed, and an industrial-size fan blew cool air across the table, cutting through the stuffiness in the room. A large, round clock over the door ticked away the seconds.

Caleb rubbed his palms on his jeans, released a tight breath and opened the folder.

For the next hour, he read and reread the arresting officer's report, the trial transcript and judge's remarks.

With his elbows on the table, he dragged his hands through his hair, then pinned his head between his arms. He tried to absorb what he had read several times. No matter how many times he reread the case, his conclusion remained the same—Zoe had paid for a crime she hadn't committed. Not technically, at least.

Pushing to his feet, he closed the folder and then wandered to the bank of windows overlooking the building's courtyard.

A man and a woman, both in business attire, shared a bench and a sandwich as they talked on their cell phones. Briefcases and pad folios lay open between them. A lady pushed a stroller outside the courthouse's wrought-iron fence. She paused at the corner, and then crossed the busy intersection, walking out of sight. An elderly man walked two large dogs, but stopped to chat with a uniformed officer.

They went about their business, oblivious to Caleb's struggle to pull in normal amounts of oxygen.

After his years on the force, he shouldn't have been surprised. Not really. He'd been called to testify in cases where the prosecuting team did everything in their power to discredit the defendant.

Sometimes the justice of the American judicial system had blurred lines.

This was one of those times.

Yes, Zoe was guilty of driving under the influence of alcohol—her blood alcohol content over the legal limit proved that. Granted, drinking and driving was stupid.

In fact, she never should have gotten behind the wheel if she had had so much as one drink.

The dude who hit her had blown through the red light and plowed into her vehicle. The impact had killed Kyle Jacoby—not Zoe's drinking.

Unless he missed something, and he didn't think he had, Zoe had spent four years behind bars paying for someone else's crime.

Prosecution had argued Zoe's impairment caused poor judgment and reaction time, leading to her conviction.

What about the guy who caused the accident? Had he been charged?

Zoe's attorney had tried to argue she wasn't at fault for the accident. Since alcohol was involved, that muddied the waters.

He couldn't do anything now to change the past, but maybe he could help Zoe release the burden she carried around and help her to realize she was worth redeeming and getting her second chance.

Maybe, just maybe, he'd get a second chance, too. But was it wise to want it with her? He couldn't risk his heart again, only to have it returned bruised and broken.

Since Zoe had left Sully and the girls at the park, she hadn't been able to get him out of her mind. And that annoyed her.

How many times did she have to remind herself the last thing she needed was to crush on her old college friend? He had enough on his plate without dealing with her baggage, too.

So, what was it about the man that kept him front and center in her mind?

She simply had to keep busy, which was why she'd

offered to help her friend Gina pack as she prepared for her move out of Agape House and into her mother's house, where her three daughters waited for her to come back home.

Agape House had been Zoe and Gina's home for the past twelve months. Zoe had left a few weeks ago, and now Gina's fresh start would begin soon.

"Mom, how do you know that guy again?" Griffin's question from the backseat pulled her away from her thoughts.

Zoe turned down the radio and glanced in the rearview mirror, her eyes connecting with Griffin's. "Which guy, honey? Sully?"

"Yeah." He nodded, then looked out the window, his brows knitted together.

What was going on inside his head? She returned her focus to the road, but tightened her hold on the steering wheel. "We were friends in college."

Sunlight flickered through the trees. She slid her sunglasses off the top of her head and settled them on the bridge of her nose.

"Did he know my dad?"

"Yes, they were roommates."

"Really? Cool. Maybe he could tell me some stories."

Sully probably had a lot of stories to share about Kyle, but she doubted if they were fitting for a nine-year-old boy. Despite having her dad and brother as solid male role models for Griffin, he missed not having his own dad around. She hated being the cause of that.

"So that's how my grandma knows him?"

"Yes." Zoe massaged her stomach, trying to soothe the residing pain. She rolled down the window to pull in a few breaths of fresh air.

"I wish Grandma wasn't so angry with you." A sulky tone coated his words.

"Honey, no matter how your grandparents feel about me, they still love you very much." At least she knew that to be true. From the moment Griffin was born, they showered him with expensive gifts—things she couldn't afford.

She glanced in the rearview mirror again to find him still looking out the open window with the wind rustling through his hair.

"Yeah, I know. They give me all kinds of presents and stuff."

Kyle had been the same way—trying to buy her love. Whenever they fought, he'd show up with expensive chocolates, flowers, or sometimes even jewelry. All she'd wanted was an apology. Or just a moment for him to really hear what she was saying.

Funny thing—about the time she had decided to end their relationship, she learned she was pregnant with Griffin. Believing a child needed a father, too, she stayed with him, hoping to work things out.

Telling her parents about her pregnancy had widened the rift between her and her father. He hadn't said it, but she could see the disappointment in his eyes. She had let him down again. At least he didn't take his feelings out on Griffin. He doted on his grandson.

Griffin leaned forward and grabbed her headrest. "Mom?"

"What?"

"You're zoning out."

"Sorry, I was lost in thought. What did you say?"

"I wanted to know what Grandma meant when she said soon she wouldn't have to settle for weekend visits?"

"When did she say that?"

"When she was talking to Sully. You were getting the drinks out of his car."

Zoe wasn't about to lie to Griffin or play dumb, but what could she say so he would understand? She puffed her cheeks and blew out a breath. "You know how you live with Grandpa Pete and Grandma Charlotte?"

"Yeah."

"Well, the Jacobys want you to come and live with them instead."

"No way! I'm going to live with you. You promised. We're going to be a family again." His voice rose as he slammed against the backseat and crossed his arms.

Tears blurred her vision, but she forced them back. She wanted to pull the car over and wrap him in a hug. "Oh, baby, we will always be a family, but yes, you are going to come and live with me."

"When?"

"Soon. I promise." And that was one promise she wasn't going to back out of. Not again. She'd simply have to make sure the courts understood she had changed. She wouldn't make the same mistakes that cost her son so much already.

"You keep saying that. Why do we have to wait?"

"Grandma and Grandpa want to be sure I'm able to be the kind of mom you deserve."

"What's that supposed to mean? You're my mom. That's enough."

"Thank you, honey. They want to make sure my job is going well so I can provide for you."

"Well, I don't know why my other grandma would say that then."

"Honey, let the grown-ups work it out. You just focus on being awesome, okay?"

"Well, I won't have to try very hard." He gave her a sideways grin.

She laughed. "No, you won't. So, after we help Gina pack, wanna go for a late afternoon swim at the lake?"

"Can Jimmy come?"

"Sure, if his mom says it's okay."

"Yes!" He thrust a fist in the air.

Would she be out of line by calling Sully to see if he and the girls wanted to join them?

Probably not a great idea. He'd said something about his sister coming today anyway. It would do her some good to keep some distance between them.

Maybe she'd give Ian and Agnes a call and see if they wanted to join them instead. They could build a fire on the beach and roast hot dogs. The boys would love that.

Right now, though, she needed to focus on helping Gina pack her things so she could leave Agape House.

As the gray-sided house with an abundance of flower-beds—thanks to June, the housemother's green thumb—came into view, Zoe slowed and turned into the driveway, parking behind Dad's truck.

"Grandpa's here."

What was Dad doing here during the middle of a workday?

She and Griffin climbed out of the car and headed for the back door, leading into the kitchen.

Dad's jean-clad legs protruded from beneath the kitchen sink. A bucket, rags and tools cluttered the floor around him.

"Hey, Grandpa."

"Hey, Griff. What are you doing here?"

"Mom and I came to help Gina pack up." Griffin stooped and peered under the sink. "What are you doing?"

"Taking a nap."

"Huh. You sure pick the funniest places to sleep."

Dad's laugh echoed in the confined space. Metal clanked against metal, then a minute later, he slid out from under the sink, holding a pipe wrench. Standing, he set it on the counter and turned on the faucet. "Hey, Griff. Look under there and tell Gramps if you see any water dripping."

Griffin dropped on all fours and stuck his head under the sink. "Nope, all good." He backed out and stood.

Dad turned off the water and started cleaning up his mess. Griffin helped by gathering scattered tools on the floor.

Trying not to let the hurt of not even a hello from Dad bother her, Zoe nodded toward the other room. "I'm… uh…going to find Gina and give her a hand packing."

She left the kitchen and headed for the living room. As she put her foot on the bottom step, her eyes lingered on the painting hanging above the fireplace.

She lost count of the number of times she'd lain on the couch in the quiet of the morning and stared at the painted image of two sets of hands—tanned, masculine ones cupping smaller milk-colored ones with a butterfly-shaped birthmark on the inner right wrist. A blue butterfly sat in the child's palms.

A father's promise to love and protect. She fingered the butterfly pendant around her throat.

"Zoe."

She turned to find Dad striding into the living room, his lips thinned and nostrils flaring.

Uh-oh. What had she done now? Her stomach turned over.

Feet apart and hands on his hips, he growled. "Why did you tell Griffin about the Jacobys' petition for custody?"

Forcing herself to remain calm, Zoe explained what had happened at the park. "I wasn't going to lie to him."

Dad rested an elbow on the banister and rubbed a hand across his jaw. "I don't think it was a wise choice."

That didn't surprise her. She couldn't measure up to his standards these days.

Instead of saying what she was thinking, she schooled her voice into a respectful tone. "I wasn't going to lie to him. The kid's smart. He picks up on things. This way we can answer questions he may have and help him deal with the situation."

"I just don't want his world turned upside down again." He leveled her with a direct look.

Again.

She shook her head, tired of walking on eggshells around him. Maybe if he knew how she really felt... Tears warmed the backs of her eyes, but she sniffed, hoping they didn't run down her cheeks and add to her humiliation. "I know I'm out of the running for Mother of the Year, but I'm working hard to rebuild my life after the mistakes I've made. I made a promise to my son that we're going to be a family again, and I'm going to do everything in my power to keep that promise, even if it means taking on the Jacobys. In the meantime, maybe you could cut me a little slack and realize I'm not a complete screw-up anymore." She turned and started up the stairs.

"Zoe, no one said anything about you being a screw-up." Dad sighed. Fatigue and resignation laced his words. "It's just—"

"You don't trust me. It's almost as if the past year has meant nothing." She tossed her hands up, tired of having the same argument with him. At least Mom could see she had changed, so why was Dad being so stubborn about it?

"That's not what I said."

"That's what you implied."

Dad waved a hand across the room. "This place has been a safety net for you, Zoe. Sure, you could come and go as you pleased, but you've been sheltered here a little bit." He jerked a thumb toward the window at the base of the staircase. "Out there…on your own…there's no one to shelter you."

"Shelter me from what?"

"People aren't always kind. They can judge you based on who your parents are and what they did. Do you really want Griffin to deal with that?" A hollow look eclipsed his eyes as his shoulders sagged.

Zoe's heart softened, realizing Dad wasn't talking about her son. She walked down a couple of steps until she could meet him at eye level and rested a hand on his arm. "I'm sorry for what you went through with your parents, Dad."

"Zoe, they passed out in a snow bank on Christmas Eve and froze to death because they were too drunk to drive home. No matter how many times they promised to stop drinking, they didn't. I spent the next eight years in and out of foster homes until I could be on my own."

"I know, Dad, and I'm sorry you had to go through

that. And I'm sorry for what I put you through. I'm sure you've had to deal with your own share of judgments because of your family."

"I wanted better for you and Ian, even if that meant making some tough choices for your own good. As your mother and I said when you left Agape House to handle your life on your own—we wanted to be sure you're ready for the demands of parenting right now. You agreed to waiting six months to get your life back on track before taking Griff back full-time."

"And I've been doing everything in my power to make the right choices, Dad. I'm not trying to reason with you to buy me a new car. This is my child's life we're talking about. Those six months may be six years to a little boy who has been begging to come and live with me again. He wants what his friends have—a family with a mom and a dad. I can't give him back his dad, but I can try like crazy to make sure he doesn't lose me again. It's my right to have custody of him again."

"I understand how you feel, Zoe, but remember—you lost that right four years ago. We are his full-time guardians right now, so let us handle the Jacobys. I promise you, we'll protect Griffin."

The door to the kitchen slammed, causing Zoe to jump and Dad to spin around.

Griffin stood in the doorway, tears trailing down his cheeks. "I hate it when you guys fight about me. I wish I wasn't even born. If they make me live with my other grandparents, I'll run away. You promised me I'd live with you, Mom. You can't break a promise once you make it." He turned and ran back through the kitchen, his feet pounding against the floor. The back door slammed, and Harper barked.

Zoe hurried down the steps, but Dad held up a hand. "I'll go talk to him."

"But—"

"Let me handle it, Zoe. I'll make sure he understands we're doing everything we can to keep the custody petition from going anywhere." Without giving her a chance to reply, Dad pushed through the kitchen door and went after Griffin.

Zoe sat on the step and wrapped her arms around her drawn-up legs as she tried to stop her body from shaking. Every time she closed her eyes, all she could see was Griffin's distraught expression. The last thing she wanted to do was cause her little boy any more pain. Now she simply had to try harder to mend his broken heart and keep her promises.

"Earth to Z." Gina snapped her fingers in front of Zoe's face. "Girl, what's going on with you today?"

Zoe blinked several times, pulling her away from replaying what happened with Griffin a short time ago. "Sorry. My mind was elsewhere."

Gina flicked her cocoa-colored braid over her shoulder and dropped the folded red sweater in the open box on her hastily made bed. "Apparently. You haven't heard anything I've said for the past ten minutes. Everything okay?"

Sighing, Zoe reached for a blue peasant blouse and folded it. "Before you arrived, Dad and I had a fight. Griffin heard part of it and got upset."

"I'm sorry, hon. Anything I can do?"

Zoe sat on the bed and twisted the folded shirt in her hands. "Unless you can turn back time, then no, but thanks."

Gina sat next to her and rested an arm around her shoulders. "Girl, if I could turn back time, neither one of us would have met because we wouldn't have made the mistakes in the first place and ended up here."

Zoe gave her friend a quick hug. "For what it's worth, I'm glad I met you."

"Me, too. Speaking of meeting…who's the hottie I saw you walking with in the park this morning?"

Zoe's head jerked up to see the smirk on Gina's face. "Sully's just a friend. And a client. What were you doing at the park? I didn't see you."

She shrugged, then pushed off the bed and shuffled to her dresser where she gathered her makeup. "Yeah, well, your concentration was elsewhere. I was…uh…heading home from work."

"How are things at work?" Zoe tried to catch her friend's gaze in the mirror and didn't like the way Gina wouldn't meet her eyes. For the past three months, she'd been working as a telephone sales agent at a local call center for a clothing distributor.

"Great." She smiled a little too brightly and leaned against the dresser, crossing her arms. "And don't change the subject."

"There's nothing to talk about, G. Sully and his daughters are clients. That's it."

"Well, he won't need your dog-training services forever. Maybe he could be more than a client." She zipped her makeup bag closed and tossed it on her bed.

Zoe dropped the now wrinkled blouse on the bed and headed for the window. She pushed it open and leaned on the sill, allowing the air to cool her face. "Yeah, well, I don't need the complications of a relationship right now.

I need to focus on getting Griffin back and having some sort of normal life."

"Normal? What's normal, huh?" Gina pulled pictures of her daughters wedged in the frame of the mirror and dropped them in a basket next to her Bible, which was coated with a fine layer of dust.

Gina's fair skin, large blue eyes and petite frame reminded Zoe of a porcelain doll—pretty to look at, but quite fragile and easily broken if handled roughly. She tempered the lecture teetering on her tongue and smiled. "You know, Gina—this is our second chance. Not everyone gets that. We can't screw it up."

Gina pulled open the top dresser drawer and scooped out an armful of socks. She dropped them in an empty duffel bag on the bed. "I hear you. Mom's been hassling me already, and I haven't even moved in yet."

"She loves you. She wants what's best for you."

Gina toyed with the zipper on the bag a moment, then looked at Zoe with vulnerability brightening her eyes. "What if I can't do this, Z?"

Zoe walked over to her and placed her hands on her shoulders. "You can. You've spent the past year preparing for a fresh start. A do-over. And you're not alone. Your daughters are cheering you on. Plus you have your mom, and you've got me. I believe in you."

"I'm not strong like you, Z. I can only hope to do half as well. You're getting your life back on track."

"It takes work, Gina, but stop selling yourself short. You made a mistake. You paid for it, and now you're doing great. Focus on being the kind of mom your girls need."

"I hate it, you know? Trying to convince the judges,

the lawyers, the world we're not losers. After a while, it's easier to believe it than to fight it."

"Oh, sweetie, I totally get that. I do, but your daughters love you. Focus on them and be the best mom you can be. It will work out, you'll see."

Even though she tried to sound hopeful for Gina, Zoe wasn't so sure she believed her own words. She talked a good game, but on the inside she was a jumbled mass of nerves. What if she lost Griffin? She couldn't deal with that. Not again.

Chapter Six

With Griffin at a friend's house, Mom and Dad out of town for some insurance dinner thing and Ian and Agnes hanging out at her mother's, Zoe had the evening to herself.

And she was bored.

She sat on the front porch in the wooden rocker built by her great-grandfather and rested her crossed ankles on the porch railing.

Thunder rumbled through the trees as spears of lightning lit up the charcoal-colored sky. Rain bulleted the lake and pounded the ground. Streams of water ran off the roof and furrowed crevices alongside the cabin. The steady patter of rain on the metal roof wasn't enough to soothe her restlessness.

The wind blew water onto the covered porch, wetting Zoe's bare feet and dotting the wooden planks. The cool moving air offered respite from the humidity that had shrouded the valley all afternoon.

Zoe pushed herself out of the rocking chair and headed inside to get a towel to dry her skin.

She stepped over Harper, who lay on a braided rug

at her feet. Harper lifted her head, then dropped it back down on her front paws and sighed.

Crouching down, Zoe ran her hand through the canine's silky fur. "I hear you, girl."

She loved the solitude of the cabin, but on days like this one, she felt isolated.

Almost…lonely.

She didn't expect her family to be her social director, but a friend to chat with over coffee would be nice. She wasn't even going to hope for a guy to snuggle up with while watching a movie or listening to the rain. She didn't deserve that.

But that didn't stop Sully's face from appearing in her mind.

Spending every day this past week with him and his girls had filled her heart with a warmth she hadn't experienced in a long time.

With Riley taking to commands so quickly, Zoe wasn't quite sure how long Sully would even need her services. The girls were doing well, and he was capable of handling things on his own.

She didn't want to call and cancel their morning classes, though. She loved that hour they spent together, even if the girls and the dog were their main focuses. At least she was with him.

But she had to stop that line of thinking. Now, if only her heart would listen…

Tired of being bored and afraid she was about to invite herself to a pity party of one, Zoe opened the screen door and headed inside the cabin with Harper at her heels.

Even with the windows open and the fans going, the cabin interior felt like a furnace.

A lingering scent of her dad's paint and solvent floated

among the exposed beams. Once she found a clean towel and dried her feet, she padded across the hardwood floor and plopped on the hunter-green braided rug in front of Mom's bulging bookcase.

A stack of books lay on top. She had promised to drop them off to the girls at Agape House.

She could deliver the books once the rain died down. Maybe she could swing by Gina's mom's to see how things were going with her and the girls. She didn't want her friend to think she was checking up on her.

For now, she'd find something to read to combat the loneliness that shadowed her evening. She pulled out a paperback and flipped it over to read the back when headlights flashed through the window and tires crunched on the gravel next to the cabin.

Harper barked and ran to the door, pawing at the wooden frame.

She wasn't expecting anyone.

She slid the book back onto the shelf and strode to the front door.

She pushed through the screen door to see Sully striding through the rain, carrying a cloth grocery bag. He climbed the steps and ducked under the porch roof. He dropped the bag on the porch, took off his baseball cap and shook the water from his hair.

With one hand bracing the open screen door and another shoved in the pocket of her shorts, Zoe tried to maintain her composure.

His hair darkened from being wet. Raindrops dotted his blue sweatshirt and faded jeans. He tugged on the hem of his shirt and used it to dry his face. Wetness dampened the hair on his exposed forearms.

He shifted his weight to his left leg and lifted a hand. "Hey."

"Sully, what are you doing here?" She stepped onto the porch, the door closing behind her.

He bent to lift the bags. "I bought ice cream, but didn't want to eat alone. Care to join me?"

"What flavor?"

"Fudge brownie delight."

"My favorite."

"I remember. Getting ice cream with you is one of my favorite college memories."

"Come on in. Where are the girls?" She stood back, holding the door open to let him pass.

He brushed past her, leaving a trail of masculine musk and the scent of rain. "Sarah took them to see a movie."

"You didn't want to go?"

"I'm sure they're ready for a break from me. Plus, Ella will be singing the songs for the next week."

"Single parenting isn't easy." Not that she'd really know. Zoe stepped away from him and headed for the kitchen. She pulled two green ceramic bowls out of the cupboard and sifted through the silverware drawer for two spoons and an ice cream scoop.

"It definitely has its challenges, but I wouldn't trade the girls for anything. My sister is a huge help, too."

"What is Sarah up to these days? I haven't seen her since your graduation. I think she was a senior in high school or something?"

"Good memory. She graduated high school a month after I graduated college. She lives halfway between here and Pittsburgh, close to my parents. She's a youth leader at a large church, working with their teen outreach program. She's engaged to the church's worship leader and getting married at the end of October." Sully wandered over to the painting of a cowboy in a canyon. "Nice painting."

Zoe set the dishes on the table and crossed the room to stand next to him. "My dad painted that last summer. Even though the cowboy is alone in the canyon with the high walls around him, I imagine his strength and endurance in facing obstacles."

"Nice interpretation." He smiled, then lifted his nose. "I thought I smelled paint or something when I walked in."

"Before I moved in, Dad used this place for his studio. Now he paints in their basement at home. Some people may be bothered by it, but it's one of my favorite smells. When I can't sleep, I come down here and lay on the couch, breathing in the scents."

"That's comforting, I'm sure."

"Things with my dad haven't been so great for a while, but here, I feel his presence, and it soothes me." She swallowed a lump in her throat and nodded toward the table. "We should eat the ice cream before it melts."

Sully unpacked the bags, revealing the cartons of ice cream, hot-fudge sauce, caramel sauce, sprinkles, crushed cookies, a jar of cherries and a can of whipped cream. And a box of waffle cones.

The spoons clattered against the bowls as Zoe set everything on the table. "Goodness, Sully, you're a dentist's dream."

"I believe in choices."

Choices. That was something she hadn't really had in a while.

She handed him the scoop. "Dig in."

"Ladies first. What's your pleasure?"

"Well, since you went to the trouble of toppings, let's go for the bowl."

"Good plan."

They made their sundaes, and Zoe filled two glasses with water. Handing one to him, she nodded toward the porch. "Want to sit outside and listen to the rain while we eat these?"

"Works for me."

Zoe led the way, holding the door open with her foot so he could pass through.

They settled in rocking chairs and set their waters on the table between them. Zoe stretched out her legs to prop her feet up on the railing again. She took a bite of ice cream and savored the velvety chocolate as it melted on her tongue.

Eating ice cream with him sent her back to her sophomore year when she and Sully had celebrated with ice cream after she'd passed her algebra class, thanks to his tutoring.

For a moment the only sounds were the scraping of spoons against bowls, raindrops on the metal roof and the jangling of wind chimes.

Sully pressed his left foot against the porch railing and used it to propel his chair into a rocking motion. He scraped up the last bite of ice cream, then dropped his spoon into the empty bowl. Closing his eyes, he rested his head against the back of the chair. "I should apologize for not calling first. After the girls left, the house was too quiet. The ticking clock in the living room sounded louder than ever and drove me nuts. Between getting the house set up and chasing after the girls, I haven't really gotten to know many people in Shelby Lake yet."

She licked hot fudge off her spoon, then set her empty

bowl on the table next to his. "No need for apologies. I'm glad you came. Even Harper was bored with just me for company."

"Somehow I doubt that." He turned and grinned, his smile blanketing her with warmth.

"If she could talk, she'd tell you." She rubbed her bare foot over Harper, who was lying at her feet. "Her sighs were getting deeper and louder."

The rich timbre of Sully's laugh flowed over her like melted hot fudge. She snuck a peek at his profile—that straight nose, square jaw, etched lines around his eyes—he had the looks of a Hollywood actor.

He stood and moved to the steps. He ran his hand down one of the support beams. "This is a great place you've got."

"Thanks. It's been in the family for over a hundred years. When I was kid, we spent most of our summers here, casting a line off the dock, watching the fireworks exploding over the lake, picnics on the beach or just rocking in one of these chairs while listening to the sounds of the forest behind us."

"I remember you talking about it. How long have you lived here?"

"A few weeks." Heat scalded her neck. She ran her thumb over her butterfly necklace. "I spent a year at Agape House, a transitional home in town for women released from prison that my parents and brother started before my release last year. When I finished the program, my parents offered to rent me the cabin until I can afford a place of my own."

Sully leaned against the railing. "It's quiet out here."

"Just the way I like it. No gossipy neighbors. No judgment. Just the lake, the trees and the bullfrogs to serenade me to sleep."

"Do you deal with that often?"

"Bullfrogs? Almost nightly."

"Yes, of course, bullfrogs."

Zoe stood and shoved her hands in the back pockets of her jeans. "I try not to let it get to me. I prefer keeping to myself so I don't cause any more shame to my family, especially my son."

"Sounds lonely." He reached out and twirled a piece of hair that had slipped from her ponytail around his finger.

She covered his hand, meaning to pull it away, but the gentle strength in his fingers and the warmth of his skin had her wanting to entwine their fingers and not let go for a long time. Common sense kicked in, and Zoe dropped her hand, taking a step back from him. "It is. At times."

"Can I ask you something?"

"Sure." She gathered their bowls and spoons.

"How did you handle it? The aftermath of the accident, the trial…prison."

She stared at the melted vanilla pooled in the bottom of her bowl. Swirls of chocolate muddied the ice cream. "I wanted to die. I hated myself for what I had done. I used to lie on the cot in my cell and think of the different ways I could kill myself."

Why had she said that?

No one knew. Not her counselor or her parole officer. No one.

Sully's probing eyes and nonjudgmental tone unlatched the lock she had fastened over the box of secrets stored in the dark corner of her mind.

He moved away from the railing, took the bowls from

her and set them back on the table. He tipped her chin up so she'd meet his eyes. "What changed?"

She hadn't shocked him with her revelation. "A woman named Jo. I attended a Bible study she offered, not expecting much. I didn't need someone else telling me I was a murderer going to hell. Jo told me how much God loved me. I told her that wasn't possible after what I had done. She reminded me about David having Bathsheba's husband killed and Paul killing the Christians. She said God could turn our pain into His gain. I called her a liar and stormed out of the room."

"What happened after that?"

Zoe rested her head against one of the support beams. "She continued to hold the Bible study, but I refused to go for a couple of weeks."

"Why not?"

"Why all the questions?" Zoe turned away from him and wrapped her arms around her waist, hoping the pressure would relieve the pain building up inside.

Sully touched her shoulder. "I'm sorry, Zoe. I didn't mean to upset you."

"I'm just not sure what you want to hear."

"The truth works for me."

Zoe scoffed and rolled her eyes. "In my experience, people don't want the truth. They want a sugarcoated tale that won't offend their sensitive minds."

"I think I can handle it." He moved closer and placed both hands on her shoulders. His voice dropped to a whisper. "Why didn't you go back for a couple of weeks?"

Her chest tightened. She squeezed her eyes shut as the truth climbed up her throat. With her back to Sully she fixed her eyes on the choppy water. "Because I couldn't wrap my head around the fact God loves me. My own father wouldn't visit me in prison. I was a huge disappointment to him. So how could my Heavenly Father love me after what I'd done?"

"Earthly fathers are imperfect. But nothing will take away God's love for you."

"Yeah, I realize that now. I went back to the Bible study, sat in the back and listened, but this time I couldn't stop crying. After the other women left, Jo prayed with me. I gave my heart to God that day." Her chin quivered. Fingering her necklace, she clamped down on her teeth until she could swallow past the thickening in her throat.

"That's really good, Zoe." He looped his finger under the chain around her neck. "Pretty butterfly."

Zoe closed her eyes and allowed a favorite memory to surface. "When I was six, my parents took Ian and me to a butterfly garden. At first, I was afraid because there were so many butterflies, and I didn't want them touching me. My dad knelt behind me and told me to close my eyes and put out my hands. I refused at first because I was too afraid. Dad put his arms around me and told me to trust him. I leaned against him and did what he said. He put his arms around mine and cupped my hands in his. He told me to open my eyes. I felt something tickle my skin. I opened my eyes to find a blue butterfly sitting on my palm."

"That's quite a moment for a little girl."

"He bought me the necklace as a reminder I could always trust him."

Serenity flowed through her like rainwater sliding off the roof. "I bet this wasn't what you had in mind when you dropped by with ice cream."

"I didn't really have anything in mind. I just knew I

wanted to see you." His mouth was so close to her ear it sent her stomach into a somersault.

Why would he want to see her?

She'd been telling herself they needed to keep a professional distance. After all, she wasn't the kind of woman he needed in his life. Was she setting herself up for heartbreak?

The smile he expected or even hoped for in response to his comment didn't happen. Didn't she want him to stop by to see her?

Caleb removed his arms from Zoe, immediately missing her closeness and the scent of her hair. He picked up the empty bowls and moved toward the door. "I'm, ah, I'm just going to set these bowls in the sink."

She turned away and moved to the side of the porch. With her arms wrapped around her waist, she stared out into the woods. "Thanks."

Thanks.

That's it.

No "I'm glad you stopped by because I wanted to see you, too."

He entered the cabin, set the bowls in the sink, cleared the table and wiped up sticky syrup. He stowed everything in her fridge, then headed back to the porch.

Zoe stood on the middle step, hands shoved in the back pockets of her jeans, and stared at the lake. Hearing him, she turned and smiled, but the playful light he had seen earlier dimmed. "Rain stopped. Wanna go for a walk around the lake?"

"Sounds good. I can burn off some of the calories I just inhaled."

Her eyes slid from the top of his head to his feet. "Calories have never been a problem for you, Sully." She lowered her gaze as a flush colored her cheeks.

Caleb raised an eyebrow and grinned as he followed her down the rutted, muddy path that led to the lake. Even taking slow, measured steps and leading with his left leg, he couldn't make the short trek without sweat slicking his skin. The heated muscles in his right thigh protested, but he wasn't about to wimp out now, especially in front of her.

He made it to the beach to find Zoe rolling the cuffs of her jeans up to keep them dry. She drew designs in the wet sand with her bare toe. Caleb stuffed his hands in his pockets and kicked at the sand with the toe of his worn deck shoe. "Did I say something back there to upset you?"

"No, why?"

"Once I mentioned I wanted to see you, you kind of shut down."

"I guess I was a little surprised by what you said. I'm not that same girl you knew in college, Sully."

"As you keep saying. I get it. And I'm not that same guy." He reached out and traced the curve of her jaw with his finger. "I've always liked you, Zoe."

"Things are so different now."

"Yes, that's true. For both of us. What happened is in the past. Don't you believe you have a chance at happiness?"

Stepping away from him, she walked to the edge of the beach and allowed the water to wash over her feet. "Honestly? No, not really."

The storm had stirred the usually tranquil water, agitating the waves sloshing over Zoe's feet. Mist rose like steam toward the sky where liquid gold fanned across the scalloped clouds, burnishing the inky lake. A light breeze tangled with Zoe's hair.

She tugged on her ponytail holder, allowing her hair to spill over her shoulders. "Can I ask you something?"

"Of course." He kicked off his shoes and toed off his socks. Seeing the vacant beach, he left them where they lay, planning to pick them up upon their return. They fell in step as they walked along the shoreline, the wet sand clinging to their toes.

"What happened with your marriage?"

He'd been expecting that question, but truth was, he wasn't quite sure how to answer.

"Once Ava was born, Val started stressing out about the dangers of my job. I totally get that, but I was a cop when she married me, you know? It wasn't like I had chosen that career on the spur of the moment." He picked up a branch that had washed ashore and used it as a walking stick. His fingers curled around the wet bark. "We fought about stupid stuff—me forgetting to take out the garbage or buying the wrong kind of bread. She resented my sleeping schedule. She'd partied in college, but after we got married, she stopped, or so I thought. She started drinking again. Things piled up. Then one night she said she wanted out of our marriage. She was tired of being a wife and mother—she had met someone else. Someone who could offer her freedom."

"I'm sorry, Sully. I can't even imagine how you must've felt. Not to mention you've wanted to be a cop for as long as I've known you."

"I don't know if you remember me telling you or not, but our family was attacked in the middle of the night when I was a senior in high school. Since then, I knew I wanted to put the bad guys behind bars."

"I do remember. It must have been awful for all of you."

"One of the worst times in my life."

"Mind if I'm nosy one more time?"

"I'll tell you anything you want to know."

"How'd you end up getting shot?"

Caleb rubbed his thigh. "Val dropped that bomb as I was heading out to work the graveyard shift. My head wasn't in the game. My partner and I had been investigating a drug ring and got a tip about a buy going down. My team raided the warehouse, expecting three guns, but a fourth guy ambushed us and started shooting. I took a bullet in the leg, but my partner was shot in the head."

If he closed his eyes, Bruce's vacant stare would materialize behind Caleb's eyelids. He worked his jaw and swallowed several times to relieve the burning in his throat. The shouting and the gunfire echoed in the murky corners of his mind. His nerves tightened as he remembered the sting in his leg followed by the fire blowing through his veins.

The other worst night of his life.

Zoe placed her hand on his arm, jerking him out of his thoughts. He jumped and fisted his hand to keep from grabbing her. "Are you okay?"

He pried his fingers open and ran a shaky hand over his face, not surprised to feel beads of sweat above his lip. "I'm fine." He sucked in a breath, then continued speaking, suddenly needing to get out the rest of the story. "I woke up in the hospital, learning I had almost died, and Bruce was gone. Once I was out of danger, Val left, leaving me with two little girls who had no idea what was going on."

"Oh, Sully…"

He rounded on her and reached for her hands, squeezing tight. An ache crimped his chest. His eyes darted around her face, soaking in every detail. "So I get it, Zoe…when you said you wanted to die. I know how it feels to be that lonely, to be that forgotten, to think no one is there for you. In one night, I lost my wife, my partner and my career."

She lifted a hand and ran the backs of her fingers on his cheek. "How did you get through it?"

"Wallowing in self-pity and yelling at God. Being a cop is what I knew, who I was. As I lay in that hospital bed with only my thoughts and bitterness for company, I cried out to God—hurt, angry and betrayed. I hit rock bottom and had nowhere to go but up. I couldn't have handled it without my sister's help."

"Apparently God had something else in mind for you."

Caleb gave himself a mental kick and a shake for turning into such a downer. He forced back the self-pity and eased into a smile. "You know what? I wanted to stop and see you, eat ice cream and maybe have a few laughs for old times' sake. I didn't mean to be such a downer."

"I'm glad you stopped by, Sully. We've both changed, yet it sounds like we have a lot in common." She released a hollow laugh. "I'm not sure if that's a good thing or not."

Caleb's eyes dropped to Zoe's mouth. He wanted to draw her close and kiss her until they both gasped for breath.

Instead he wrapped his arms around her and pulled her against his chest.

She hesitated, then leaned into his embrace.

Zoe ignited a spark in Caleb's heart. Like lighted tinder in a forest, the feelings he buried years ago for Zoe burst into flames and nearly consumed him. Common sense would tell him it was too soon, but after what they'd both experienced, they couldn't afford to wait. Now all he had to do was convince her they both deserved to be happy again.

Chapter Seven

Why did Zoe volunteer to cover Leona's Kids & Canines training class?

Other than working with Griffin and Sully's daughters, she didn't have any experience teaching kids. But she understood animals, so how hard could it be? Really?

Besides, Leona had enough on her plate, being awakened early this morning with news her mother had had a stroke.

When Leona called to say she and Travis were headed out of town and asked Zoe to cancel the class, she heard herself volunteering instead.

Housed in the basement of Canine Companions, the large training center gave the dogs plenty of space to run and exercise their muscles. Sunshine poured in through the narrow windows at ground level and reflected off the polished tile floor. Painted paw prints decorated the cement block walls. The agility training equipment had been pushed to one end of the room so the students could focus on their own training instead of messing with the weave poles, jumps and crossbars.

Children, ages eight to twelve, raced around the room,

laughing and calling for the barking, excited dogs to chase and play with them.

She pulled in a deep breath and smoothed down her royal blue Canine Companions polo shirt. She could do this.

Moving to the middle of the room, she held up her hands to get their attention. "Hey, everyone. Welcome to Kids & Canines training. Parents, if you and your child will guide your dog to one of the individual paw-print mats, we'll get started."

Parents corralled their kids and their dogs and did as Zoe asked. Once everyone found a colored mat, she smiled and cleared her throat. Now twenty-one pairs of eyes—seven children, seven adults and seven canines— stared at her.

"Dogs are such a wonderful part of your family, so it's important you know how to behave with your furry friends. Leona had a family emergency this morning, so I will be filling in for her."

The side door opened, and Sully hurried in with Ava in his arms and holding on to Riley's leash while Ella skipped along beside him.

Her eyes widened as her heart tripped up her throat.

What was he doing here?

He set Ava down and, holding on to both girls' hands along with the dog's leash, he guided them to the empty paw-shaped mat. Ella waved to her. "Hi, Zoe."

Zoe waved, but words melted on her tongue.

Sully gave her an apologetic smile. "Sorry we're late."

"No worries. We're glad you could join us."

He must have gotten a haircut within the last week because a strip of lighter skin edged his hairline. Could those girls look any cuter in their matching watermelon-pink shirts, green leggings and lopsided ponytails?

Pulling her gaze away from his family, she returned her focus to the rest of the group and resumed her introduction. "My name is Zoe James, and I've been on staff at Canine Companions as a dog handler for almost a year."

A woman, who had been ignoring others, including Zoe, by talking on her phone, paused her conversation and held up a hand. "Wait a minute. Did you say your name was Zoe James?"

"Yes, ma'am, I did." Zoe didn't recognize the blond-haired woman dressed in a turquoise short-sleeved peasant blouse, cuffed white shorts and wedge sandals.

The woman ended her call and stowed her phone. She dropped her hands to her hips. "When I signed my daughter up for this class, I expected Leona, not some… Well, you."

The woman's sneer and sharp words speared Zoe's soul like a verbal bayonet. Heat scalded her neck and set her face on fire as her heart ratcheted against her rib cage. Her chest heaved as she forced air into her lungs.

Keep it together. Remain professional.

Drawing in a deep breath, Zoe counted to five under her breath, and then spoke. "Ma'am, as I said, Leona had a family emergency early this morning. If you'd prefer to reschedule your daughter's training for a different time when Leona is available, I'll be sure to let her know, and she will contact you as soon as she is able."

"Yes, that's what I'd definitely like to do." The woman reached for her dog's leash and propelled her daughter toward the door. "Come along, Ashlyn. We'll come back when a *real* trainer can help us."

Sully's eyes narrowed. He took a step forward, but Zoe

flashed him a quick look, begging him with her eyes not to do anything. His lips thinned and a muscle jumped in the side of his jaw, but he gave her a slight nod to let her know message received.

They started for the door, but then the woman turned and addressed the rest of the group, who watched the exchange with wide eyes and open mouths. She made a circling motion with a manicured nail. "The rest of you may want to reconsider scheduling once you realize who she really is and what she's done."

The parents whispered between one another while their kids watched with confusion coloring their sweet faces. One of the dogs whimpered and rested his head on his paws.

Zoe dropped her gaze to her feet and forced back the lump forming in her throat.

Ten minutes ago, she had been excited about this possibility. When she offered the suggestion to Leona, her boss had given her blessing. Without even an opportunity to demonstrate her abilities, the chance to prove herself had been snatched away by one critical parent.

A warm hand touched her arm. She didn't need to open her eyes to know Sully had approached her. "Zoe? You okay?"

She wanted to stalk out of the room, slam the door, or at the very least bury her face in his chest and release the emotions pummeling her breastbone. But she couldn't do any of those things.

She needed to remain calm. No matter how much it hurt.

She locked eyes with Sully. The concern lining his face nearly had her throwing herself at him. "I'm fine."

But she wasn't. Not really, but she needed to show she could be professional in the face of disaster.

Another woman stepped forward. Instead of heading for the door like Zoe expected, she stalked across the room to the woman bent on leaving with her daughter and dog. She flicked her blond ponytail over her shoulder and folded her arms over her chest. "Pam, if you want to leave, then go, but stop causing unnecessary trouble."

"Trouble? Do you know who she is? What she's done?"

"Yes, I've known Zoe for years. I'm thankful she was willing to give up her Saturday to fill in for Leona at the last minute, because that's what she's done. Anything else you may or may not be referring to is in the past. Where it belongs." The woman's frosty tone left little room for argument.

Pam glared at her, then at Zoe. Instead of pouring out more verbal acid, she pushed her daughter through the door, slamming it behind her. The child's cries bounced off the cement walls outside the training room.

Zoe ached for the little girl having a mother with such a horrible attitude. Apparently second chances weren't acceptable in that family.

Silence blanketed the room. Not even the dogs stirred. Zoe puffed out her cheeks and emptied her lungs. Steeling her spine, she faced the rest of the group. "I'm so sorry about that. Perhaps it would be best if we postponed this class until Leona is able to teach again."

The woman who had confronted Pam stalked to the middle of the room and wagged her finger in Zoe's face. "Nuh-uh. Zoe James, you are not going to let Pam Turner beat you down. Time to shine, sweetheart."

Pam Turner? Who used to be Pam Jacoby, one of Kyle's cousins? Seriously?

Acid eroded a hole in the pit of her stomach, causing any remaining courage to leach out.

Zoe took in the woman's sleek ponytail, large hoop earrings and lithe body of a runway model. Then recognition popped the light bulb in her brain.

How could she not recognize her high school friend Holly Matlin? They'd been joined at the hip from their freshman year until graduation, much to her parents' dismay. They felt Holly had been a bad influence by encouraging Zoe to party.

But right now she was a much-needed ally.

"Thanks, Holly, but I'm not the right person for this class. I'm sorry for wasting everyone's time."

"Girl, you've never been a quitter, so don't start now. I've heard you're some kind of dog whisperer. Show these people what you've got." Holly threw an arm over Zoe's shoulders. "Maybe after class we can grab some coffee and catch up. That is, if that hottie with the two adorable girls doesn't claim you first. He hasn't taken his eyes off you since he walked in."

"Sully. He's a…friend."

"He seems like a very nice…friend." Holly gave her a knowing look and grinned as she moved back to her mat being saved by a boy around Griffin's age and a fluffy butterscotch-colored Pomeranian.

Forcing Pam's exit from her mind, she focused on the group. She showed a quick video on safety rules and pets. Then, for the rest of the hour, she showed them how to train their dogs to sit with the help of positive reinforcement and small treats while appealing to the canines' five senses. She moved from family to family, offering one-on-one help.

As she approached Sully and the girls, she slowed her steps so she didn't appear eager.

Sully knelt beside Ava and encouraged her to speak the "sit" command to Riley. Ava curled her arm around Sully's neck and buried her face in his shoulder as she shook her head. He sighed, but didn't pressure her.

Ella bounced in front of the pup. "Remember how Zoe taught us at Daddy's house, Avie?" Ella held her hand out to Riley, who sniffed it. Then she commanded him to sit. The pup dropped on his back haunches. She smiled, clapped her hands, then fed him the treat and rubbed his head as he gobbled the biscuit. "Good boy, Riley."

"Wonderful job, Miss Ella." Zoe held out her open palm, and Ella slapped her five.

Keeping her tone neutral, Zoe glanced at Sully. "I'm surprised to see you today."

His smile created crinkles around his eyes that she'd been getting used to seeing. "You, as well. You were a great trainer, but I figured a group setting like this would be good for the girls, and it would help with Riley's attention and socialization. I didn't count on this nice surprise."

She knelt and petted Riley. "He's doing well."

"I've missed you this week."

Zoe stood and brushed dog hair off her shirt as Sully's words seeped into her soul and smoothed over the jagged edges that had kicked off the class. She tucked her hands under her arms to keep from brushing his hair off his forehead. "It's been a busy week, but I've missed you, too."

"The girls and I are roasting marshmallows tonight. How about if you join us for s'mores?"

Roasting marshmallows and making s'mores with her

family had been one of her favorite childhood memories. She hadn't done it in forever. The idea appealed to her until she remembered her weekend plans with her son.

"That sounds like fun, but I'm picking up Griffin after class. He's spending the night with me."

Sully shrugged. "No problem. Bring him along."

Sully had met Griffin already at the park, but this get-together would be different. No dog training. Just hanging out. What did that mean for their relationship? Did they even have a relationship beyond friendship? Maybe in her dreams…

He needed his head examined. Why else would he invite Zoe over tonight when the place was a wreck? She was going to think he was a complete slob who couldn't keep it together.

He gathered Ella's fairy-princess wings and wand, capped three of Ava's markers and kicked one of Riley's toys over to his basket.

Riley barked, picked up the stuffed hedgehog in his teeth and scampered under the coffee table to chew on the squeaky toy.

Caleb carried the girls' things to their room, which looked a lot worse than the living room. Stuffed animals, babies, plastic dishes and broken crayons littered the carpet.

He gathered their overflowing hamper and headed for the laundry room. He had thrown in a load of towels before the Kids & Canines class, but they needed to be put into the dryer.

As he reached for the laundry room door handle, giggles sounded on the other side of the closed door.

He turned the knob and opened it. Ella and Ava

splashed barefoot in a large puddle growing out from under the washer.

Seeing him standing in the doorway, both girls froze, their eyes wide.

"What's going on, girls?" He struggled to keep his voice calm.

Ella waved him in. "Come in, Daddy, and splash with us."

"Where did the water come from, Ells?"

"It just appeared."

Caleb dropped the hamper, splashing water on his feet, and headed for the washer. He opened the lid and lifted one of the wet towels. The heavy material dripped way too much water.

Beautiful.

He slammed the lid, causing Ava to jump.

He smiled to assure her everything was okay. "Sorry, Aves. Daddy didn't mean to make you jump." He placed his hands on their shoulders and guided them out of the room. "Let's get your feet dried and maybe you can help Daddy get this place cleaned up before Zoe comes over."

"Yay, Zoe's coming. Did you hear that, Avie? Zoe's coming." Ella clapped and danced down the hall into the living room.

Caleb dropped on the edge of the couch and buried his face in his hands. A washer full of sopping-wet towels thrilled him about as much as a root canal. With it being Saturday, he'd pay an arm and a leg getting a service person out there.

The girls needed baths before church in the morning. Towels would be quite helpful for that.

Wait a minute...didn't Baxter, a colleague from his

previous squad, mention something recently about his washer when they talked last? Caleb remembered his friend mentioning the washer not spinning out and having to take his uniform to the Laundromat.

Caleb fished his phone out of his jeans pocket, thumbed through his contacts and found Baxter's number. He slumped on the couch while the phone rang.

"Sullivan! What's up, dawg?"

"Hey, Bax. How's it going?"

"You know—same ole, same ole. How's it going out in the sticks?"

"Well, it has its moments."

"How are the girls?"

"Good. Good. Growing like weeds. Hey, man, remember last year when your washer bit the dust and wouldn't spin out?"

"Oh, yeah. Why?"

"Well, the same thing just happened to me. Got any ideas before I shell out some bones for a weekend service call?"

"Sure, man. Could be the drive belt, motor coupling or lid switch assembly."

Caleb groaned. "None of those sound like quick fixes."

"If it's the motor coupling like mine was, you can fix it yourself. There's a website I used that gave me step-by-step directions."

"Let me grab a pen." Caleb padded into the kitchen and scrounged in one of the drawers for a pen. He found a grocery store receipt and flipped it over. He uncapped the pen with his teeth. "Okay, go. I'm ready."

Baxter rattled off the site, and Caleb scribbled the address. "Thanks, man. That's a huge help."

"No problem. Hey, while I got you on the phone, I heard something you should know."

By Baxter's tone, Caleb suspected he wasn't going to like what his friend was about to share. "What's up?"

"I ran into Valerie."

Caleb pressed his back against the counter and ran a hand over his face. He was right. "Yeah? How's she doing?"

"She's remarried."

His friend's words were an invisible punch in the stomach. Caleb's jaw dropped as he tried to catch his breath. "Wow. No kidding."

"Sorry, dude."

"No worries. She's the one who decided she didn't want a family." An ache pinched his chest.

"Yeah, about that..."

"What?"

"She's pregnant."

Caleb nearly fell over. His fingers gripped the phone as he struggled to find words.

"You okay?"

"Yeah." His words wheezed out through clenched teeth.

"Sorry to be the bearer of bad news."

"Don't sweat it."

They ended the call. Caleb dropped the phone on the counter, then slid down the front of the cabinets and landed on the floor. With his elbows resting on his knees, he dragged his hands through his hair and squeezed his eyes shut against the tears pricking the backs of his eyes. He ground his jaw. His ragged breath came out in shuddered gasps.

She'd had a family and turned her back on them. What

right did she have starting a new one? What was wrong with him? Or their beautiful daughters, for that matter?

Would he ever be enough?

Chapter Eight

When Zoe picked up Griffin and asked if he'd like to hang out at Sully's, he was all for it. Any reservations she had disappeared about ten minutes after they arrived. He took to Sully like he'd known him all his life.

Sully tossed a football to Griffin, then praised him when he caught it.

Something about seeing Griffin and Sully together stirred a sense of love she hadn't experienced in years, if ever.

What she was beginning to feel for Sully wasn't anything like what she had felt for Kyle.

Although he was Griffin's father, Kyle had never really committed to his paternal role. Sometimes he'd acted like Griffin had been more of an annoyance.

They were both young, and her pregnancy had thrown them for a loop. Had he lived, maybe he would have grown into being a father. Because of what she had done, though, Griffin wouldn't ever know his real dad.

Watching Sully and Griffin together made her realize just how much she longed for this kind of relationship for her son.

She was certainly getting ahead of herself by placing Sully in that position.

Zoe snuggled deeper into the sweatshirt she'd borrowed from him and rubbed her chin on the collar, inhaling his masculine scent. She pulled her feet up to the edge of the lawn chair and wrapped her arms around her legs.

For the moment, the events of the day disappeared as contentment swaddled her like a cozy blanket.

Sully had built a fire a couple of hours ago. She had snapped a few pictures with her phone as he'd helped Ella and Ava toast marshmallows to a golden brown and sandwich them between chocolate and graham crackers.

A piece of wood snapped and shifted, sending a shower of sparks toward the treetops. Tendrils of smoke spiraled over her head. Twilight stroked the sky with shades of mauve and navy.

Ella ran around the yard trying to cup fireflies in her small hands. Ava followed, dragging a well-loved blanket behind her. She stopped to rub her eyes.

Zoe pushed out of the chair and crossed barefoot to her. Evening dew dampened her toes. She stopped in front of Sully's youngest.

Zoe pushed Ava's hair away from her face. "Hey, sweetie. Are you getting tired?"

Ava nodded and popped her thumb in her mouth.

"Want to cuddle with me?"

Ava hesitated, searched the yard until her gaze settled on Sully, then she nodded again.

Zoe lifted her and carried her back to the chair. She cradled Ava in the curve of her arms and wrapped the bedraggled blanket around her. The pink shirt she'd worn to the training class this morning was smudged with chocolate.

Ava's eyes fluttered a minute before closing. Within seconds, her breathing relaxed.

She kissed Ava's head and breathed in the scent of her baby shampoo mingled with the sugary sweetness of the melted marshmallow sticking to her cheek.

A yearning she hadn't felt in a while tugged at her heart. It had been so long since she had held Griffin like this.

Now he had started fourth grade. Where had the time gone?

She peeked over the fire at him. Instead her gaze tangled with Sully's. An expression she couldn't quite make out flickered over his face. He said something to Griffin, who glanced at her and nodded.

With the football tucked in his arm, Sully jogged across the yard to her. Griffin stooped to help Ella catch fireflies.

Sully dropped the football on the ground and dragged a chair next to hers.

His eyes roamed from the top of her head to the tips of her feet. Then a slow smile spread across his face. "My sweatshirt looks good on you."

Warmth spread across her face.

"So does my daughter." He brushed Ava's curls off her forehead and leaned over to press a kiss to her soft skin.

Inches from her face, Sully caressed Zoe's cheek. "I'm glad you came."

"Me, too." Her breathing hitched as he watched her with darkened eyes.

His thumb traced the curve of her bottom lip as his eyes lingered on her mouth.

If she leaned forward just a—

"Daddy! Look! Griffin caught a firefly." Ella bounced

over to him and tugged on his arm. "Can we have a jar? Please, Daddy?"

Sully jerked up and nearly tripped over his chair as he jumped to his feet. He scrubbed a hand over his face before turning to Ella. "Yes, sweetie. I'll find a jar for you."

Zoe bit the inside of her cheek, but it wasn't enough to hold back the giggle tickling her throat.

Sully leaned over and whispered in her ear, his voice low and husky, "The next time I think about kissing you, there will be no interruptions. I promise you."

She stifled a shiver and locked in on his words— *next time*.

Caleb Sullivan wanted to kiss her.

He turned and strode into the house. He returned a moment later with a jar and a fleece blanket. He handed the jar off to Griffin, then spread the blanket out beside Zoe's chair. "Why don't you lay Ava here? It's got to be killing your back, holding her like that."

"It's not that bad, but she may be more comfortable if she can stretch out." Zoe leaned forward to pass her to Sully.

Ava batted at Zoe's arm. "No, Riley."

Zoe froze, and Sully's head jerked up. "Did you hear that?"

"Yes."

Grinning, Sully laid her on the blanket and covered her up with an opposite corner. "Maybe there's hope for her yet."

"She hasn't spoken a single word since Valerie left?"

"Not one, but I've always known she'd speak when she's ready. I've made an appointment with a specialist now that we're somewhat settled."

"I'm glad you're feeling settled. From what you've said, this past year has been tough on you."

"Yes, but we're managing." Sully stifled a yawn.

Zoe pulled back her sleeve to check the time. "Maybe Griffin and I should go so you can get the girls inside and into bed."

"Getting the girls to bed isn't a bad idea, but I don't want you to leave. Ella still has plenty of energy to burn off." He nodded to Griffin kneeling in the grass beside Ella as they filled their jar with lightning bugs. "Griffin's a great kid. He's very patient with my little chipmunk."

She smiled. "Thanks. I think I'll keep him."

Sully dropped in the chair next to Zoe. For a moment, they listened to the crackling of the fire, the night sounds and Griffin's low tones talking with Ella.

"When Ian and I were little, we used to catch fireflies."

"I think it's a rite of passage during our childhoods."

"Yes, I agree. My mom didn't appreciate me releasing them in Ian's bedroom, though."

Sully laughed. "I'm sure she didn't. We don't have many nights left to see them. Soon it will be too cold."

He stretched an arm over the back of Zoe's chair. His fingers stroked her shoulder. "Would you like to go to dinner sometime?"

"Just the two of us?"

"Yes."

She peered at him by the light of the fire. "Do you think it's a good idea?"

Sully leaned forward and tossed a small log on the burning embers, and used a paper plate to fan the flames. "Actually, yes, I think it's a great idea, which is why I brought it up."

Zoe wanted to say yes. So what was holding her back? "Sully…"

He pivoted to look at her. "Look, Zoe, I know we both have a lot going on in our lives right now, but the truth is—I like you. I don't believe our meeting up after all these years was a coincidence. I believe God brought us together for a reason. What's the harm in taking things slow and seeing where they lead?"

The harm was she could end up losing her heart to the one guy who should have had it all those years ago.

Caleb's head and heart battled with casualties on both sides.

He was a walking contradiction.

His heart begged him to call Zoe and reassure her they'd be great together. Then his head pulled him back with reservations about their pasts colliding with their futures.

He stoked the burning embers. A swirl of smoke stroked his nose. He dropped in his chair and burrowed deeper into his fleece pullover. The night air chilled his face, but he wasn't ready to call it a night. He picked up the sweatshirt Zoe had borrowed off the empty chair and breathed in her lingering fragrance mixed with smoke.

Riley followed him outside and jumped in his lap. While Caleb stroked his silky fur, he pondered the past few hours.

The evening had gone better than expected, especially after Baxter's bombshell had left him reeling for the rest of the afternoon. He'd stumbled through the house like a zombie, but managed to pull it together before Zoe and Griffin had arrived. He didn't tell Zoe what he had learned because, quite frankly, he didn't want it to cast a shadow over their evening.

He rested his head against the back of the chair and stared at the stars glistening against the sooty sky. Fatigue seeped through his bones.

He tried not to let the disappointment from Zoe's lack of commitment to his request for dinner filter through his thoughts and discourage him.

Maybe he shouldn't have said he liked her. At least, not yet. That was kind of stupid, considering he still had reservations. Even though he meant it, he struggled against those feelings because he didn't want to make the same mistake twice.

Not just with giving his heart to someone else, but falling in love with someone who had been involved with alcohol.

But Zoe wasn't like Val.

No, she seemed to have overcome her past and had goals in place for her future.

He respected that.

God did bring them together again, so what did he have to do to convince Zoe they should at least see where this relationship could go?

"Hey, what are you doing sitting out here by yourself?"

Caleb turned to find his sister, Sarah, walking through the yard. "Where'd you come from? I didn't hear you pull up."

"I parked in the driveway, looked for you inside, checked on the girls and came out here. The back door was open." She leaned down and gave him a one-armed hug, then held both hands over the fire.

"My attack dog didn't even stir." Riley stirred long

enough to see who was talking, then dropped his head back on Caleb's thigh. "I left the door open to listen for the girls."

"Blame it on my superior ninja skills." She grinned, the fire casting half her face in shadows. She wore jeans and a pink hoodie.

"Yes, I'm sure that's what it is. So what brings you by so late?" He nodded toward the empty chair. "Have a seat. You cut your hair."

She pulled her fingers through her straight hair cut to her chin. "Yeah, time for a change, I guess."

Sarah dropped into the same chair Zoe had used. She leaned forward and rested her folded arms on her knees. "Mind if I crash with you for a few days?"

"Of course not. What's going on?"

"Adam and I broke up." Her voice caught. She dashed a hand across her cheek, then fingered her bare ring finger on her left hand. "And I quit my job."

Caleb sat up, nearly dumping Riley off his lap. "Seriously? Your wedding is in six weeks."

"For reals. Apparently he decided he's not ready for a commitment of this magnitude." She made air quotes around the last few words. "I couldn't stay with the outreach program because he's so heavily involved in it, too."

"I get that you're hurting, and for that I'm very sorry, but can we agree not to use phrases like 'for reals'? It's up there with 'totes' and 'adorbs.'"

"Ahh, the middle schoolers getting to you?"

"The kids are great. Their language... Wow, I feel like such an old man."

"To them, you're practically ancient, dude."

"Yeah, don't remind me." He turned and looked at

her. "Seriously, though, Adam's an idiot. How are you handling everything?"

Shrugging, she pushed her chair against his. Then she sat and rested her head on his shoulder. Her chest shuddered. "We were together four years, and he broke my heart. I've cried for two days, but I've decided I've wasted enough tears on the jerk. Maybe love isn't all it's cracked up to be. Mom and Dad fight constantly about Dad's long hours and Mom's spending. Not exactly stellar role models for marriage. And Val walked out on you."

Caleb slung an arm around her shoulder, and then dropped a kiss on the top of her head. "Just because my marriage fell apart, that doesn't mean your love life is doomed."

She smacked his arm with the back of her hand and wrinkled her nose. "Ew. Can we not call it my love life? That sounds like something Grandma would say."

Caleb laughed. "What do you want to call it?"

"How about my relationship?"

"Fine. Don't base your future relationships on your family's failures."

"I think that's great advice for you to take, too, big brother."

"It's been a rough year."

"I know, but don't allow the shadows of your past to cloud your future, Caleb." She stood and poked one of the leftover marshmallows onto a stick and pushed it into the coals. "Speaking of future, how's Zoe the dog trainer?"

He stared into the flickering fire as the flames raced across the logs. Crickets serenaded them from their hidden depths in the grass. "Fine."

"That's it? Fine?" She pulled out her flaming marsh-mallow and blew out the flames.

"What do you want me to say?" He leaned forward, resting his elbows on his knees, and clasped his hands. He wasn't quite ready to share his feelings about Zoe with anyone, especially his baby sister.

She shrugged, pulled the marshmallow off the stick and shoved it into her mouth. "I don't know. How do you feel about her?"

"We're friends."

"But?"

"But what?" Caleb leaned back and rubbed a hand over his jaw. "I like her, okay? Happy now?"

"I knew it." She didn't try to disguise the cocky tone in her voice. "Your tone changed when you said 'fine.'"

"It's not that simple, though." He stood and kicked a burning log closer to the core of the fire, sending a shower of sparks into the air.

Sarah's chair creaked as she settled back into it and licked her fingers. "Why not? You're single. She's single. Go for it."

"She's in a very vulnerable place right now, and I'm not going to take advantage of that." He shoved his hands into his front pockets. "Remember Kyle, my college roommate?"

"Vaguely. Wasn't he killed in a car accident or something?"

"Yes, and he was also engaged to Zoe. She's a friend from Bartlett. She was driving the night Kyle was killed. Alcohol was involved, and she spent four years behind bars."

"Are you serious?" Seeing he wasn't joking, she shook her head. "Oh, the irony—the cop and the ex-con."

"Enough, Sarah."

"What are you doing hanging out with her?" She swatted him on the arm. "Why didn't tell me about her past sooner?

He frowned and held up a couple of fingers. "One, I know her, and she deserves a second chance. And two, it's not really any of your business, is it?"

Sarah tossed her hands in the air. "Caleb, don't be an idiot. She took somebody's life. You really want someone like her around your daughters?"

He ground his teeth. He wasn't in the mood to fight with his sister, especially since she was hurting, but he wasn't going to let her rip into Zoe. "You don't know her, so don't even start judging her. She's had enough of that already. She's broken up about what happened and carries that guilt every day. She has a kid who is growing up without a father."

"Whoa. Are you serious?" Sarah jumped to her feet and grabbed his arm. "Oh, Caleb, what are you doing?"

He shook off her hand. An ache formed at the base of his skull. "At the moment, staring at the fire and wishing this conversation never took place."

"Didn't you have enough drama with Val? Do you really want that kind of relationship again? By the way, didn't you get into some trouble at your old job because of some of Val's antics? "

He held up a hand. "Look, I appreciate your concern, but I know what I'm doing."

She scoffed. "I've heard that before."

"Low blow, Sarah. Zoe is nothing like Valerie. She doesn't even drink anymore."

"I love you, and I don't want to see you hurt again."

Sarah slid an arm around his waist and rested her head on his shoulder.

He dropped an arm around her shoulder. "What makes you think Zoe's going to hurt me?"

"What makes you think she won't?"

He couldn't think of an answer to that, and maybe that's what bothered him the most. But he couldn't help but remember Zoe from the early years. Yes, they'd both changed and grown, but deep down where it mattered, they were the same people. And that's what he was banking on.

The last thing he wanted was to subject his daughters to more heartache, but his gut told him Zoe wasn't going to hurt them the way their own mother had.

"You're not answering, so that makes me wonder if you're not already concerned about it."

Caleb moved away and reached for his chair to fold it. He was so done with this conversation. "Of course I'm concerned. What about you? You spent four years with a guy who decides six weeks before the wedding he's not ready for such a commitment. Does that mean you're going to wrap your heart in bubble wrap and store it in the attic?"

"Interesting metaphor." Sarah reached for her chair and folded it.

"You know what I mean."

"Yes, but my situation was different. I don't have two darling girls to worry about."

He took the folded chair from her. He strode to the deck and leaned them against the railing. "Zoe has done nothing but treat the girls with love and respect. She's very gentle and patient with them. They adore her."

Sarah crossed her arms over her chest. "So if you don't

see a future with her, then maybe you need to break ties now before they get in too deep. If things don't work out with you and Zoe, then those little darlings are going to be heartbroken all over again. You can handle it, but can they?"

Chapter Nine

The stench of cheap perfume and yesterday's booze saturated the air. Staring at Gina passed out on the ripped and stained couch, Zoe had no choice but to make the call. It was the kind of call she couldn't take back.

If anything happened to Gina, Zoe had no one to blame but herself.

When her friend called last night from The Sassy Cat and begged her to come down, Zoe refused. She wanted nothing to do with the seedy lounge on the edge of town known for bar fights, drug deals and worse.

But the strands of fear tangled with desperation in Gina's voice had pushed Zoe to find her keys and confront her friend in the dimly lit parking lot adjacent to the bar's lot reeking of stale beer and emptiness. She simply couldn't violate her sentencing agreement by stepping onto the property, couldn't risk her freedom, or destroy the trust she'd built with her family to follow her friend inside the bar.

Last night's confrontation looped over and over in her head. No matter how many times she replayed her conversation with Gina, she couldn't help but feel like she should have done more. She begged Gina to come home with her, but her friend insisted she had no choice.

Since leaving Agape House about a month ago, it hadn't been as easy for Gina. The last time Zoe talked with her, Gina mentioned the struggles of living with her mother, how her coworkers whispered behind her back, how the girls went to their grandma instead of to her. She believed the kind of people inside The Sassy Cat offered her more grace than the ones who attended church on Sundays.

But Zoe knew they didn't. They took what she was willing to give away, even her newly found pride and self-respect, but Gina refused to see it that way. And look where it got her.

Now Zoe had Gina's daughters to consider. The three girls—ten-year-old Savannah, seven-year-old Daisy and four-year-old Lucy—huddled together in the overstuffed floral chair that probably looked great in the '80s and watched her with large eyes edged with fear. Canned laughter from some program on TV echoed in the background.

How would their lives be affected if her call caused their mother to go back to jail for violating her parole?

She paced, stepping around a pile of crayons dumped by an open coloring book, a half-dressed Barbie doll, an assortment of multicolored rubber bands and a loom that littered the floor, along with empty fast-food wrappers, dirty dishes and a pile of clothes overflowing from a broken clothesbasket.

Gina needed help, and right now, Zoe was the only logical person who could make that happen.

She had no choice. She had to make the call.

She pulled her cell phone out of her pocket and tapped Mom's name in her list of contacts.

"Hello?"

"Mom, I'm at Gina's. I need you."

"What's going on?" A guarded tone filtered through her words.

Zoe glanced at the girls and kept her voice low. "Gina needs help."

"I'll be right there."

"Wait…she's not at the same place. She's in a trailer across the street from The Sassy Cat."

"What… Never mind. I'll find out more once I get there."

Zoe ended the call and stowed her phone.

Once Gina was sober again, she'd probably be furious, but she had her daughters to consider, too.

Zoe knelt in front of the chair and reached for Savannah's hands. "Savannah, honey, how long has your mom been sleeping?"

"She wouldn't wake up when it was time for us to go to school. What's going to happen to her? Will she go back to jail? It will be all my fault if she does." Tears rolled down the girl's face.

"No, sweetie, it won't. You did the right thing by calling me. I called my mom. She will know what to do."

"Van, is Mommy going to die?" Lucy folded her hands on the arm of the couch and rested her head on her fingers.

Zoe lifted the little girl, sat on the floor and cuddled Lucy in her lap. She finger-combed a tangle out of Lucy's matted curls. "Your mommy isn't feeling very well right now. She's sick, but she's not dying."

Please, God, don't make a liar out of me.

Daisy sniffed and rubbed a hand over her eyes.

The girls needed to be in school, laughing and playing with their friends. Not stressing about their mother's fate.

How did they end up in this disgusting trailer, not even fit for wild animals?

"Savannah, where's your grandma?"

"She and Mom had a big fight, and Mom left. Mom made us go, too. We didn't want to, but Grandma promised we'd be able to come back to her soon."

"Why did you call me and not your grandma?"

She shrugged, and then chipped away at the purple nail polish on her thumb. "I don't know. Mom really likes you. I guess I didn't want her mad if she woke up and found Grandma here."

Already at ten, Savannah had learned how to do damage control. That weighed too heavily on Zoe's shoulders.

Did Griffin do that for her? Did he make excuses to his friends? Did he try to play peacemaker within her family?

"I'm glad you called." Zoe smiled and patted the girl's knee.

A knock sounded on the door.

Zoe set Lucy back on the chair, then stood to answer the door. Her mother waited on the narrow metal steps. Zoe stepped aside and let her through.

Dressed in her trademark trousers, white blouse, pearls around her neck and with her hair pulled back in a clip, Mom looked out of place, but that didn't prevent her from kneeling on the grungy carpet and flinging her arms open.

"Miss Charlotte!" All three girls leaped off the chair and ran into her embrace.

Mom held them tightly against her chest, not caring

if their tears and runny noses ruined her clothes. She glanced at Zoe with worried eyes.

"Miss Charlotte, I'm so sorry. I didn't know what to do." Savannah threw out her arms as a tortured expression marred her pretty face.

Mom rubbed a thumb over her cheek, chasing away a stray tear. "Sweet girl, why are you sorry? You did exactly what you should have."

"What's going to happen to Mommy?" Daisy's quiet voice trailed off as she stared at Gina sprawled on the couch.

"Honey, we will take good care of her." Zoe's mother stood and dusted off her pants. She eyed the clock, and then looked back at the girls. "Have you had breakfast yet?"

They shook their heads.

She cupped Savannah's cheek. "How about if you find your sisters something to eat?"

Her shoulders slumped. "We're outta milk and cereal."

"What do you have?"

"Bread and peanut butter."

"Peanut butter toast is one of my favorites for breakfast. How about helping your sisters get their hands washed? Would you mind making them some toast?"

Savannah shook her head.

"You're a wonderful helper."

"Come on, Lucy and Daisy." Savannah wrapped her arms around her sisters' shoulders and led them into the filthy kitchen, where dishes piled in the sink and an open trash bag spilled onto the floor.

Once the girls were out of sight, Mom hurried to the couch and shook Gina's shoulder, calling her name quietly, yet firmly. When she didn't respond, she pressed her fingers against the inside of Gina's wrist. She looked at Zoe with alarm in her eyes. "Her pulse is weak. We need to get her to a hospital right away."

"Alcohol poisoning?" Zoe kept her voice low so the girls didn't hear.

"I don't know. I'm going to call an ambulance, then I'll get in touch with Gina's parole officer." Mom strode over to the door where she dropped her purse and pulled out her phone.

"Is that necessary?"

"Yes. See if you can get ahold of Wilma so she can come and get the girls." Her mother tapped 911 into her phone and spoke to the dispatcher.

Zoe headed into the kitchen and forced herself not to gag at the smell emanating from the sink. She swallowed several times, then moved into the dining room where Savannah made toast for the girls. "Savannah, honey, do you know Grandma Wilma's phone number?"

Savannah cut a slice of toast in half and handed one to each of her sisters. "No, she had to get a new phone because Lucy dropped hers in the tub. The number is probably in Mom's phone, though, but I don't know where it is."

"It was an accident, Van." Lucy's lower lip trembled.

Zoe caressed the top of the girl's head. "No worries, sweetie. We'll find it." Sure the girls were set, Zoe returned to the living room and relayed the information to her mom. "What about the girls in the meantime?"

"Call Ian and Agnes. They're approved for emergency foster care. They can take the girls until we can figure out how to get in touch with Wilma."

"I'll see if I can get some clothes and things put together for them. I'm not sure if anything's clean."

"We can get a load of clothes washed." Her eyes surveyed the mess on the floor. "Better yet, don't worry about it. Agnes keeps clothes on hand for emergencies, and I can pick up a few things for them."

Sirens wailed in the distance.

Zoe needed to call her brother, but the need to confess her previous involvement propelled her to act before the ambulance arrived. She clutched her phone. "Mom, there's something you should know. I was at The Sassy Cat last night."

Mom's eyes bulged. Her shoulders dropped as she shook her head. "Oh, no, Zoe. Please don't tell me that."

Zoe held up a hand and rushed to say, "I didn't go in. I stayed in the parking lot next to the bar. I wasn't even on the property."

"You shouldn't have been even that close." Disappointment laced Mom's voice, which made Zoe regret her actions all the more.

"Gina called and sounded so desperate. I thought if I could talk her into coming home with me, then I could help her."

"Why didn't you call me?"

"I didn't want her to get into trouble." Now the excuse sounded lame, but truly she meant well. "You don't know what it's like, Mom. Going back to jail will wreck her."

Mom reached for Zoe's arm. "That's not up to you."

"No, maybe not, but I totally understand what she's going through."

"But you're getting your life back on track. You're so responsible now."

"And I wanted the same thing for Gina."

Mom pushed her hair away from her face the same way she had done for Savannah. "It's not your job to save her. Leave that up to God. It's your job to love her and to show her grace."

"But you did…you saved me." Zoe covered Mom's hand with her own.

"No, honey, God did. I prayed every night and asked Him to save you, no matter what it took."

Zoe pulled their hands away from her face and traced Mom's elegant fingers. "I'm sorry."

Sirens split the air. Flashing lights swirled through the front window, casting a red glow on the floor.

"I know, honey. The ambulance just pulled in the driveway. Let's get Gina stabilized, then we'll get this mess sorted out." Mom started to pull away.

Zoe grabbed her hand, suddenly desperate to be understood. "No, Mom, I mean I'm sorry for everything." Her eyes filled as her chest heaved. "That could easily be me lying there. I'm so sorry for what I've put you and Dad through."

"My darling girl, what happened is in the past. Learn from it, and move forward." Mom pulled her into a quick hug, but broke away when a knock sounded on the door.

Mom hurried to open it. Two EMTs dressed in gray uniforms entered, carrying emergency kits. Their radios squawked.

The girls rushed into the living room, their eyes large and tear-filled. "Is Mommy going to jail?"

"No, sweeties, she's going to the hospital for a checkup." Zoe gathered them closed and herded them down the hall to one of the bedrooms. They didn't need to see Gina strapped to a gurney. She turned on the TV and shifted the girls' focus to an educational cartoon. She quickly dialed Ian's number and spoke to Agnes in hushed tones, who promised to come right away.

Her phone trilled, signaling a text—from Sully. She read it:

Free for dinner tonight?

Sorry, something came up. Not sure when I'll be home. Call u later?

Sure. Hope all is well. Looking forward to talking to you. Miss you. <3

Her heart somersaulted at his last words.

Despite the drama in the living room, she couldn't help but smile. For the past couple of weeks, they'd spent their evenings watching movies together, taking walks, talking around the campfire and getting to know one another all over again.

They've both changed a lot since college, but Zoe had no problem remembering the old Caleb. This older, more mature Caleb had improved with age. He was the exact kind of guy she'd always wanted in her life.

Was her heart willing to take the risk?

Supposedly go-karting was like riding a bike, except he hadn't gone go-karting in over ten years. Not since that night at college with Zoe for her birthday.

Tonight, he wanted to put a smile on Zoe's face. When she showed up at his door, upset about a friend in trouble, it was all he could do not to pull her into his arms and kiss her sadness away. Maybe he would have if Sarah and the girls hadn't been there.

After introducing Zoe to Sarah quickly, his sister offered to watch the girls while he spent some time with

Zoe, but she cautioned him to be careful. He cautioned her to chill out. And trust him. He knew what he was doing.

"So the loser buys the ice cream?" Zoe slid into the red go-kart in front of his.

"That's been the tradition, if you count one time as tradition."

"Works for me. Eat my dust, Sullivan."

"You talk tough, James. We'll see when you're paying for my triple scoop."

Lakeside Pins & Spins had very few customers, but since it was a weeknight, he wasn't surprised. The indoor recreation park boasted a go-kart track, bowling alley, arcade and a small pizza place and ice cream shop. Apparently, on weekends, especially during the colder months, the place was a zoo.

Colorful racing sponsors decorated the red walls. The stench of fuel exhaust lingered in the air. Bright overhead lights illuminated the smooth track.

The track attendant wearing shorts and a red-and-yellow jersey stepped alongside his go-kart and yanked on the pull cord to start the engine. Then he moved ahead and started Zoe's.

Their engines roared, echoing off the high ceilings and sounding like twenty running lawn mowers parked in his living room.

Zoe pulled out of the gate and accelerated onto the track. He pressed his foot on the gas and raced past her, giving her a thumbs-up as he went by.

Taking his eyes off the track for a moment, he didn't see the turn in time to ease off the accelerator. He stepped on the brake a little too sharply and spun around. She veered around him, laughing as she rushed past him.

The sound took him back to the days of midnight pizza runs, walking Zoe home after tutoring, and celebrating her successful exams with ice cream. Back when life was less complicated.

For a moment, he paused to remember the night he had taken Zoe go-karting after Kyle ditched her on her birthday to sneak around with someone else. Despite his roommate's attempts at secrecy, Zoe had found out. Wanting to cheer her up, especially on her birthday, he suggested going for a walk. His fresh-faced friend hadn't known he had fallen in love with her. He'd kept that secret to himself.

Her ponytail had been pulled through a bright pink hat, and she'd worn a light gray fitted T-shirt. They had walked into town and ended up at an indoor go-kart track. He'd always admired her sense of adventure, her willingness to try something new.

Afterward, he'd bought her ice cream. They'd walked home, and it was all he could do not to kiss her goodnight. Despite how he felt, he wasn't about to make a move on his friend's girl, even if his friend had behaved like a jerk.

Zoe zoomed past again, pulling him out of the past. "Come on, slowpoke!"

He righted his go-kart and pressed the accelerator.

They spent the next fifteen minutes looping the track, trying to outrace one another.

They returned their go-karts to the attendants, then headed for the ice cream shop. Zoe licked her chocolate-ripple cone with a smirk on her face while Caleb paid for their ice cream.

He didn't mind losing to her.

He grabbed a napkin and wiped chocolate off the corner of her mouth. He would have preferred kissing it off, but he didn't want to make her uncomfortable.

Grabbing her hand, he pulled her toward the door. "Let's head outside. I need to air out my brain after smelling those fumes."

They left the shop and walked through the lobby of the recreation park.

Zoe stopped and turned back to face the shop. "You know what? I'm going to run back to grab a bottle of water. Want one?"

"Sure." He reached for his wallet.

She put a hand on his arm. "I got it."

She disappeared inside the ice cream shop. He sat on the bench next to the doorway to the bowling alley. The thunderous crashes of balls against pins echoed out into the lobby. The scent of grilled hot dogs caused his stomach to gurgle, despite the cookie-dough cone in his hand.

He didn't even think to ask Zoe if she had eaten. Maybe they should grab a quick bite.

"Sullivan, what are you doing here, man?"

Caleb looked up to find his neighbors Shawn and Pam Turner and their daughter Ashlyn exiting the bowling alley.

Caleb's eyes darted toward the ice cream shop. He willed Zoe to stay inside. He didn't need Pam's claws to mark up her heart again. Since the dog-training class, he'd kept his distance from his neighbors. "I'm here with a friend. What about you guys?"

"I had the night off, so we decided to play a couple of games." Shawn jerked his head toward the bowling alley.

Pam looked over Caleb's shoulder and sighed. "Oh, not again. I've spent months avoiding that woman, and now I've seen her twice in the same month."

Caleb turned, and his heart sank. Zoe came out of the ice cream shop carrying two bottles of water.

Zoe caught them watching her. Her feet slowed, and instead of coming toward them, she changed course and headed for the front door.

Enough was enough. He wasn't going to allow her to feel she needed to run and hide.

"Zoe, wait." He glanced at the Turners, who watched him with narrowed eyes. "If you'll excuse me…"

Shawn snaked out a hand and gripped his upper arm. "Dude, why are you hanging out with her? Do you know who she is?"

Caleb shrugged off his arm, then tossed his melting cone in the trash next to the bench. He wiped his hand on his jeans. "Of course I do. She's my friend."

"You need to choose better friends. You know about her past, don't you?" Shawn jerked a thumb toward the door.

How many times did people have to ask that? He wasn't an idiot. And this was a small town. "Yes, but that's exactly what it is—her past. She's not the same person."

"How do you know?"

"Because I know her." When was she going to catch a break?

Pam pushed past Shawn and faced Caleb, her hands fisted on her hips. "She killed my cousin."

This was getting out of hand way too quickly.

Caleb held up a hand. "Pam, listen, I'm very sorry for what your family endured. It was a horrible tragedy, but should this woman pay for the rest of her life?"

Tears filled her eyes as her lower lip trembled. "Do

you know what it's like to have someone you care about taken from you?"

Yes, yes, he did.

Caleb stuffed his hands into his front pockets and shifted his feet. "My partner was killed because of a choice I made. I have to live with that for the rest of my life. I guarantee a day doesn't go by without Zoe thinking about what happened, but come on, the woman can't be tarred and feathered for this for the rest of her life."

"Tell that to my aunt and uncle, who are spending the rest of their lives without their son." She stabbed him in the chest with her finger. "Come on, Shawn, let's go. I'm no longer in the mood for ice cream."

As they pushed through the door, leaving behind a trail of disgust and recrimination, Caleb dropped onto the bench and dragged his hands through his hair. Not only did he have to work with Shawn, but he lived next door, too. If he kept seeing Zoe, would he have to move? Find a new job? The last thing he wanted was to uproot the girls, but he didn't want to give up on Zoe, either.

Even the crisp autumn night air couldn't cool Zoe's scalded cheeks. Her blood rushed through her veins as she strode across the brightly lit parking lot. Reaching the street, she paused, realizing she had two options—walk home in the high heeled boots she had worn for style or do an about face and slink back inside with a target on her forehead. She'd had enough of Pam Turner for one night.

If only she had met Sully here instead of leaving her car parked on the street in front of his house and riding with him. Maybe she could call Ian and Agnes for a ride? No, she didn't need anyone else to witness her humiliation. She'd walk the few miles back to the cabin, then figure out a way to get her car from Sully's. She wasn't a stranger to walking. So she'd have a blister or two tomorrow. That was nothing compared to the wounds on her heart.

Sighing, she trudged down the road, making sure to stay on the gravel. Dressed in dark washed jeans and a black leather jacket over her red sweater, she didn't exactly stand out to traffic. She tried not to let her imagination run wild over the rustling in the bushes to her right. The tree branches hanging low swayed and swatted at her. The wind picked up, and she pulled her jacket tighter around her waist.

Keeping her head low, she forced one foot in front of the other, seriously doubting her sanity at that moment. Something dropped on her hair. She brushed the top of her head only to have another drop hit her hand.

Thunder cracked, startling her. Lightning flashed, lighting up the blackened sky. Half a second later, rain showered her.

Perfect ending to a lousy day.

Pulling her coat over her head, she sprinted down the street.

Headlights from an approaching vehicle swept the glistening surface. Instead of passing her by with a splash, the car veered off the roadway, spitting gravel as it staggered to a stop in front of her. The driver's side door flew open, and Sully jumped out. He strode her, a thunderous look etching his face.

He swept her into his arms and crushed her to his chest. "Thank God, you're okay."

Arms pinned to her sides, Zoe struggled against his constricting hold. "No thanks to you." She pushed free and moved past him.

He grabbed her elbow. "What's that supposed to mean?"

"Nothing. Forget it. I just want to go home." She shook off his hand.

"Zoe, wait."

She ignored him and continued for the edge of town where lighted sidewalks offered relief from the uneven gravel path.

Uneven footfalls scuffed the stones. "Zoe, stop!" Sully's heavy breathing made her pause. She glanced over her shoulder to be sure he was okay only to see him stumble and fall, coming down on his right knee. He cried out. The sound—a cross between a wail and a yell—sent a shiver down her spine.

She turned and ran back to him, illuminated by his headlights. "Sully, are you all right?"

"Do I look all right?" He growled as he shifted to sit on the wet ground. With his head bent and arms quivering, he forced his right leg to stretch out in front of him. He sucked in a short breath.

She touched his shoulder. "Sully, I'm so sorry. What can I do?"

"Nothing. I have to wait for the throbbing to stop enough so I can stand and put some weight on it."

Guilt flooded her. If she hadn't acted like an idiot and pushed away from him, this wouldn't have happened.

Jagged shards of lightning zipped over the trees. Thunder rumbled as the wind picked up.

"We can't stay here, Sully. Lean on me. I'll help you to the car and drive you home."

He heaved a breath, rubbed a grimy hand across his forehead, and then braced his weight on his arm as he pushed himself up. His eyes bulged as he shifted his legs. He teetered to one side.

Zoe rushed to slide her arm under his and placed her hand on his shoulder. "Use me to walk. I can handle it."

They shuffled to the car. She pushed away long enough to open the passenger side door. He dropped on the seat, gritted his teeth and lifted his injured leg inside, his chest heaving.

Zoe slammed the door and jogged around the front. She slid behind the wheel, trying to ignore the wet seat from Sully leaving the door open. After adjusting the seat and mirrors, she shifted the engine into Drive and headed to Sully's.

She glanced at him, only to find his head resting against the window and a hand covering his face. A muscle jerked in the side of his jaw. Deep lines bracketed his taut mouth. Returning her eyes to the road, she mentally kicked herself for being so foolish.

She turned into Sully's driveway and shut off the engine. He had the door open and was already trying to get out before she could even unbuckle her seat belt. She hurried out of the car and to his side. Sliding her arm around him, she braced her leg to support his weight.

They reached the front door, but before Zoe could open it, it flung open.

Sarah stood in the doorway wearing navy flannel pants and a white hoodie. She held a bottle of crimson nail polish in her hand. She locked eyes with Zoe, then shifted her gaze to Sully. "Caleb, what happened?"

"I fell."

She pushed the door back, shoved the nail polish in her pocket, and then positioned herself on the other side of Sully. The scent of popcorn lingered in the air. Riley barked and danced around their feet.

"Down, Riley." Zoe and Sully commanded in unison.

Riley dropped on his back legs and cocked his head, his tongue hanging out of his mouth.

The three of them staggered into the living room where a bowl of popcorn sat on the coffee table and a sitcom played on the TV. Zoe pushed an afghan out of the way and removed her arm from Sully's shoulder so he could ease onto the couch.

He dropped his head back on the arm of the couch and sighed, closing his eyes. Zoe moved to his feet and untied his shoes, dropping them on the floor.

"What happened?" Sarah sat on the coffee table and touched the hole ripped in Sully's jeans, exposing a two-inch gash crusted with dried blood and bits of gravel.

With eyes still closed, Sully waved a hand toward her. "Zoe, my sister Sarah. Sarah, this is Zoe."

"You introduced us already." Sarah's eyes did a slow slide from the top of Zoe's soaked head to the tips of her muddy boots. Her mouth tightened, then she said, "So, you're the one."

What was that supposed to mean?

The knot tightened in Zoe's stomach. She forced a smile. "Nice to see you again."

Sarah said nothing in return, but focused her attention on her brother. "You need to get some ice on that knee."

"Yeah, I'll get right on that."

"Glad to see your sarcasm wasn't injured in any way." Sarah stood and left the living room. Zoe could hear the chinking of ice scraping together, and then the faucet turned on.

She returned with a plastic bag full of ice wrapped in

a dishtowel and a glass of water. Zoe stayed rooted on the end of the couch while Sarah placed the bag carefully on his knee. She held two small pills out to him and a glass of water. "Here, take these."

Sully opened his eyes and pushed himself up with his elbows. "What are they?"

"Your pain pills."

He tossed them back and guzzled the water. Handing her the empty glass, he gave her a tired smile. "Thanks, sis. Now beat it, would ya? I need to talk to Zoe without an audience."

Sarah reached for the remote and shut off the TV. Then she picked up the popcorn bowl and shot her a look Zoe couldn't interpret. "Fine. I'll be in my room if you need anything."

She ran a hand over her tangled hair. Heat climbed up her neck. Nothing like making a great impression...

As soon as Sarah left with Riley in tow, Sully struggled to a sitting position, resting his injured leg on the coffee table. Beads of sweat broke out on his upper lip.

Zoe wanted to do something, anything to help relieve his pain, but she'd done enough. In fact, she should probably just leave before she caused any more trouble for one day.

She pushed to her feet and glanced toward the front door. "Sully—"

"Stay."

The single word spoken with fatigue, yet, maybe just maybe a hint of longing was nearly her undoing. Tears filled her eyes. She swallowed several times until she could speak without making a fool of herself. "I'm sorry. You're hurt because of me."

He patted the cushion beside him. "Sit with me."

She shrugged out of her leather jacket and tossed it in the chair. She sat on the edge of the cushion next to him and turned to face him. "I'm so sorry for your leg."

Sully tugged on her arm, pulling her off balance. He leaned forward and wrapped his arms around her, dragging her closer. Her face pressed against the softness of his long-sleeved T-shirt. She breathed in the scent of his soap and listened to the rhythmic beating of his heart.

He traced the curve of her cheek, then tipped her chin up so he could meet her eyes. "Why did you leave?"

She dropped her hands and tried to rub the grime from her fingers. "I couldn't stay and cause a scene. I wouldn't embarrass you like that. I waited outside, but when you didn't come, I figured you'd had enough."

"Well, you figured wrong. I didn't follow you because I was too busy sticking up for you."

"You stood up for me? Why?"

"Zoe, you know what your problem is?" His gentle tone softened the sting in his words.

She couldn't help but feel defensive. No one really wanted to know their flaws, did they? "I'm sure you're about to tell me."

"You're too quick to run." He tucked a lock of hair behind her ear. "You need to stand up to these people instead of feeling sorry for yourself."

Zoe reached for his hand and pulled it away. The more he touched her, the harder it was not to bury herself in his arms. Right now she didn't think that would do either of them any favors. "That's easy for you to say. You didn't kill anyone."

"Not directly, but my choices cost my partner his life."

"Your partner was killed by someone else's bullet."

"And your fiancé was killed by the car that ran the

red light. Your blood alcohol level just exacerbated the situation."

"How did you know that?"

"I read your case file."

"You spied on me?" She jumped to her feet and fisted her hands on her hips.

Sully threw up his hands and shrugged. "I'm a cop, Zoe. I wanted to know the facts."

"You could've asked me." She wrapped her arms around her waist, feeling sick to her stomach.

Sully removed the ice from his knee and moved to his feet. He grasped the couch for support. "No, I would've gotten the 'it's all my fault' version."

"It was my fault. I shouldn't have been drinking and driving."

"No, you shouldn't have. But there were other circumstances in that case."

"Yeah, well, the jury thought differently. No changing that."

He placed his hands on her shoulders and leveled her with his no-nonsense cop face. "Maybe not, but you don't have to slink around town like a coward afraid to stand up for herself. Think about what kind of example you're setting for your son."

She hadn't thought about it that way. All she wanted was to keep her head down so she didn't bring any more shame on her family. Instead, she ended up looking like a coward. Was that really how Sully saw her?

"We've got a problem."

"What's that?"

"My presence in your life is going to cause problems with your neighbors." She jerked a thumb toward the Turners' house.

"I'd rather get new neighbors than lose you." Sully cupped her face in his hands. Then he pulled her into his arms.

As much as his words warmed her heart, she couldn't help but wonder if Sully realized how much he'd have to sacrifice with friends and maybe even his professional relationships by associating with her. Was she willing to do that to him?

Chapter Ten

Even with the sunshine warming her face and the pleasant air blowing in off the lake, Zoe couldn't stop the shiver that ran up her spine. She rubbed her arms briskly to generate some heat. Maybe she should have worn pants instead of the black-and-white-patterned skirt that matched her short-sleeved black sweater.

The color was fitting for her emotional state after what had happened with Gina and then what happened after go-karting with Sully. Her heart hung heavy in her chest over the events of the past couple of days. She spent as much time as she could at the hospital, but trying to talk to Gina left both of them frustrated. Her friend wallowed in self-pity instead of trying to work through her problems.

Waking up in the detox unit of the hospital hadn't helped matters, either. But Gina had no one but herself to blame for the choices she made.

Zoe talked with her own counselor to realize she couldn't do any more until her friend wanted the help.

The only thing she could do was pray for Gina and her family. The rest she'd have to surrender to God.

Gina's slide back into her old life made Zoe even more determined to prove she could be the woman she longed to be. Since she left Agape House, she had maintained a full-time job, paid her bills on time and kept her weekly appointments with her counselor and parole officer.

She wasn't going to end up like Gina.

Griffin wasn't going to wake up one morning and find his mother unconscious from alcohol poisoning… or worse.

She'd win her parents' trust, regain custody of Griffin and live the life God intended for her.

Which meant surrendering to Him daily because she was weak and couldn't do it on her own.

And after talking with Sully the other night, she needed to work on acquiring a backbone so she didn't look like a coward to her son.

Maybe she could begin right now.

Squaring her shoulders, she turned away from the lake and headed for the Lakeside Chapel, the stucco building that had sat on the edge of the campground for nearly eighty years.

Despite her growing relationship with God for the past couple of years, sometimes Zoe felt like a fraud stepping inside the Lakeside Chapel. But then she had to remind herself she had been redeemed for the past sins that had kept her enslaved. Sometimes she had to remind herself several times a day, especially when she ran into people like Pam Turner who treated her like a leper.

But she wasn't going to let what happened the other day at the go-kart track color her worship this morning. She needed the time to let go of some of her anxieties and soak in the pastor's sermon.

Zoe recognized a few faces as she walked into the

simple, clean sanctuary that smelled of lemon oil and fresh air. Twin stained glass windows on either side of the pulpit cast a rainbow hue across the polished hardwood floor.

She slipped into one of the bench-style pews in the back row and smoothed the wrinkles out of her skirt. A cross breeze fluttered through the open side windows, ruffling her hair. She turned her face toward the window and closed her eyes, breathing in the crisp scent of new beginnings. A dog barked in the distance, competing with the mellow sounds of the prelude.

As people filed into the sanctuary and filled the pews, they nodded, smiled or acknowledged her with a hello. Some of the faces looked familiar, as she'd seen them around town. They recognized her—she could tell by the expressions on their faces—but they still greeted her warmly.

Maybe she could feel welcome here, find a home church where she belonged.

Since returning to her hometown, the church she had attended as a child with her parents didn't offer her the same sense of welcome she'd once experienced. She attended because of Griffin, but instead of feeling the presence of the Lord, she felt censure. Since the Turners attended there, she didn't need to have another run-in with Pam, so she chose the small chapel up the road from her cabin.

"Zoe?"

She turned at the sound of her name.

Holly Matlin, her old high school friend, stood behind her, her dark hair held back by a yellow headband that matched her yellow cardigan. She carried a little girl about nine months old on her hip.

"Hey, Holly. What are you doing here?"

Laughing, she batted a hand at Zoe. "Same as you—attending church."

Zoe stroked the little girl's hand. "Oh, yeah, right. Is this little cutie yours?"

"Yes, this is Isabella. She's ten months today. I had my son, Trenton, at your Kids & Canines class. I think he's in the same class as your son?"

"Could be. I'll have to ask Griffin." A sense of failure filled her for not knowing her son's friends' names or who his classmates were. She'd do better by getting involved. When she went to her parents' tonight for their weekly Sunday dinner, she'd ask him about school.

"How are you? I wanted to catch up with you after that class, but your attention was directed elsewhere." She winked.

Sully and his daughters.

"Thank you, by the way, for sticking up for me. I appreciate the support."

"I've never been a fan of bullies, especially those who think they can throw their name and money around to get what they want. We really need to catch up."

Zoe placed a hand on her friend's arm. "Please don't take this the wrong way, Holly, but we were friends during a time of my life that doesn't hold great memories for me. Our partying—well, my partying—caused my family a lot of pain. I'm not that person anymore, and I can't risk falling back into that same lifestyle." The image of Gina's unconscious body floated into her thoughts.

Holly reached over the pew and gave Zoe a quick hug, surprising her. "Oh, honey, I'm not that same girl, either. Life has a way of smacking you upside the head with a wake-up call called reality."

"Tell me about it."

"I met a guy who gave me a choice—partying or him. After a heavy tug-of-war in my heart, I married him and haven't looked back. I'm Holly Dempsey now."

"Sounds like a great guy."

"He's perfect for me."

"Maybe I'll take you up on that catch-up session and get to meet him."

"You can meet him today. He's preaching." She pointed to the back of the small church where a man in his early thirties dressed in khakis and a polo shirt shook hands with an elderly gentleman. "I need to find my son and find our seat. I'll catch up with you soon."

As Holly hurried down the aisle to corral her son and get seated, Zoe remembered how much fun Holly had been, even when they weren't drinking.

It would be good to catch up. She'd finally have a friend. And a pastor's wife at that. Maybe Holly would be a good one to talk to Gina, to show her it was possible to put that damaging lifestyle behind and focus on one filled with promise and hope. Zoe made a note to seek Holly out after the service.

Pastor Dempsey walked to the front of the sanctuary, welcomed the congregation and introduced himself. He opened with prayer, then directed everyone to open their hymnals.

As she searched for the number, someone slid in beside her and tugged on her skirt.

She looked down to find Ella smiling up at her. Sully held Ava's hand as she moved in by her sister.

"Hey, girls," she whispered, then looked up to find Sully smiling at her. Her heart jumped, and she couldn't stop the smile spreading across her face if she tried.

He wore black pants and a red checked dress shirt with the sleeves rolled up to the elbow, exposing tanned, muscular forearms. He leaned over and whispered in her ear. "You look beautiful. I've missed you."

The warmth of his breath near her ear sent a tremor shimming through her. "I missed you, too."

And she did. She hadn't seen him in a couple days—not since the night they had gone go-karting. As much as she wanted to talk to him, she needed a little distance. Time to put things in perspective, perhaps? She tore her gaze away from his eyes and shared her hymnal, trying to focus on the words without much success. She hadn't seen him in several days, and all she wanted to do was stare and drink in the sight of him.

The rich timbre of his voice harmonized with hers as they sang. Her heart soared to hear him worship beside her.

By the time they finished singing and moved into the pastoral prayer, Zoe relaxed. Having Caleb sitting next to her, his arm brushing against hers, filled her with a sense of completion. Peace settled within the recesses of her soul. Even the songs about God's love and grace acted as a balm, soothing the myriad of emotions she'd experienced this past week.

Caught up in her own thoughts, Zoe missed the scripture reference Pastor Dempsey had shared with the congregation before he started reading. She peeked at Caleb's open Bible, which had all kinds of notes written in the margins, and then turned to Ephesians.

Pastor Dempsey closed his Bible, holding his place with his finger. He paused, made eye contact with the congregation, and then asked, "The Bible tells us we've been saved by grace, but I ask you—how far does grace go? Does that give us license to sin? Is grace a safety net? Or does it mean God's supply is limitless and we need to go to Him daily for that day's portion? Also, do we expect people to show us grace, yet hesitate to extend the same grace to others who've wronged us? No matter what we've gone through, we're reminded in Isaiah that we have been redeemed. God knows us by name. We are His."

Tears pooled in Zoe's eyes, blurring the words on the page. She dabbed at her eyes with her fingertips.

Conviction about her decisions rooted her to her seat. She'd been so guilty of expecting grace from her hometown, but she was quick to put up her guard when it came to showing grace to others like the Turners. Same with the Jacobys. They'd lost a son because of her involvement, yet she expected them to embrace her with compassion?

When was the last time she had prayed for them? Had she ever?

Sully reached for her hand and gave her a gentle squeeze. She gave him a watery smile. As she listened to the rest of the sermon with Sully's hand covering her's, she realized Caleb was right—God had brought them together for a reason. God had set her on a path for a second chance, not only with Him, but also with Caleb, a man who knew about her past and cared about her in spite of it.

The Bible didn't specify the apple as being the forbidden fruit, but Caleb could understand why Adam would be tempted if Eve offered one to him. He sunk his teeth into the speckled buttery-yellow Golden Delicious and allowed the tangy sweetness bathe his mouth. He swiped a hand across his lips and took another bite.

When they arrived at Newman's Orchards, August

and April Newman invited them to sample some of yesterday's pickings.

The tractor hitched to the wooden wagon trundled down the rutted path, carrying them to the apple orchard. Sunshine warmed his face as his back pressed against the side of the wagon. Ella sat on his left leg, and Ava curled in Zoe's lap while Griffin snuggled between Caleb and Zoe. He stole a glance at Zoe to see her enjoying her apple, too.

Talk about being tempted. He wanted to lean over and press a kiss to her lips, but he wouldn't. Not in front of the kids.

Besides, he needed to figure out what direction this relationship was going, especially after his run-in with the Turners at the go-kart track the other night.

Yeah, he could understand their pain and anger—if he was in a similar situation, he'd probably feel the same way. He was human.

But couldn't they see Zoe wasn't like that? That what happened was a tragic accident and not premeditated?

So, how was he supposed to continue building a future with the woman he loved while living next door to and working with Turner? Would he have to think about moving? Uproot the girls now that they were beginning to feel settled? Change careers?

Should he back off? Maybe he should've thought of that before he opened his big mouth and invited her and Griffin to join them at the orchard, but after not seeing or talking to her for a couple of days, he missed her.

Thinking about it tightened his gut.

Pastor Dempsey's question this morning—how far does grace go?—had him questioning some of his own fears. What if things progressed with Zoe, and she slipped back into that old lifestyle? What if she chose the bottle over him? How would he handle it? He didn't just need to worry about himself, but also the girls. They'd already been through their mother's abandonment. They were becoming attached to Zoe, so if something happened, their little hearts would be broken again. Could he fix them a second time?

But Zoe'd shown she had no interest in that former life. She'd made great strides to prove she wasn't what her past sins portrayed.

The confusion gave him a headache.

He needed to release the struggle. It wasn't up to him to control the outcome. His job was to rely on God and allow his faith to see him through whatever may come their way.

The fragrant breeze ruffled their hair and rows of trees dotted with red and gold grew taller as they approached. The tractor stopped, causing the wagon to jerk. Caleb tightened an arm around Ella.

"Daddy, you're squishing my breath."

"Sorry, chipmunk. I didn't want you to fall off my lap."

"Well, if I did, you'd just pick me back up again, right?"

"Yes, Ells, I would. You can count on that." He dropped a kiss on the tip of her freckled nose.

Mr. Newman stopped the tractor at the edge of the orchard and climbed down. He circled to the back of the wagon to lend a hand with the passengers needing assistance off the walk. Besides Caleb's group, two other families with small children had chosen today to spend time together at the orchard.

Griffin jumped down. He was quick to help with Ella. Zoe grabbed a wooden picnic basket and a plaid blanket while holding on to Ava's hand. Once Caleb eased off the wagon, he reached for Ava and set her by her sister, and then he took the basket, setting it on the ground. Then he reached for Zoe's hand. Once her feet touched the ground, though, he wasn't ready to let go.

She leaned into him, close enough for him to smell her perfume. "You okay?"

"Yes, why?"

"You were scowling in the wagon."

"Oh. Just trying to work out a problem in my head."

"Come up with an answer?"

"Yes, I realized it wasn't my problem to work out. I needed to let it go." He dropped an arm around her shoulder. "So, if I pick enough apples, will you make me a pie?"

She elbowed him in the side. "I was going to ask you the same thing. You're really getting a handle on the domesticated-bliss thing."

He smiled down at her and longed to share what was in his heart. Instead he ran a finger along the curve of her jaw. "Sometimes I think I need to have all the answers when what I really need is just to get through that particular day. At times, it's definitely a challenge, but we're getting into the swing of things. You've been a huge help as we've gotten settled here. It's really beginning to feel like home."

"I'm glad." She threaded her fingers through his and squeezed.

Over her shoulder, he caught sight of Griffin watching them, his eyes staring at their joined hands. Caleb released her fingers, making a mental note to catch Griffin when they were alone to see what was going through the boy's head. How did he feel about seeing Caleb holding his mom's hand?

Caleb got the opportunity to check in with Griffin sooner than he'd expected.

About ten minutes into their picking, Zoe helped Ella and Ava fill their small bags. Caleb moved next to Griffin who was jumping to try and touch an apple on a lower branch.

"Need a hand, bud?"

Griffin grunted as his feet left the ground again. His fingertips nearly brushed the tips of the leaves. Caleb stretched and pulled the branch down low enough for Caleb to grip the apple. He tugged on the fruit, and the branch snapped back.

"Got it. Thanks, Sully." Griffin grinned and thrust the apple in the air like a trophy.

Caleb clapped him on the back. "Way to go. Want to help me fill my bag?"

"Sure." Griffin stooped to tie his shoe, then ran ahead to where Caleb had been picking apples.

Caleb pulled branches low enough for Griffin to grab the apples. "Hey, Griff, mind if I ask you a question?"

Griffin shrugged. "Yeah, I guess."

"How do you feel about me hanging out with your mom?"

Griffin plucked another apple, but instead of setting it in the basket, he tossed it from hand to hand. "I don't know. It's okay, I guess."

"You guess? Does it bother you?"

"No, I guess not. My mom smiles when you're around. I like seeing my mom smile."

He did, too. He'd do whatever it took to keep that smile on her face.

As if to prove her son's point, he glanced at Zoe to see her watching them. She lifted her hand and waved. He waved back, then returned to picking apples with Griffin. While they filled their basket, Griffin filled him in about school and his friends.

One of the girls cried out behind him. Caleb spun around. Spying Ava on the ground with Zoe crouched in front of her and Ella sitting beside her, he dropped the apples in his hands and hurried over to his daughters.

"What happened?" He crouched beside his daughter and wiped her tears with the hem of his shirt.

Zoe uncapped her water bottle and poured it over the cut on Ava's little knee. "She was running and tripped on her untied shoelace. She skinned her knee."

Caleb sat on the ground and pulled Ava into his lap while Zoe tended to her wound. He dropped a kiss on the top of her head. "Are you okay, princess?"

She nodded.

Ella wrapped her arm around her sister's shoulders. "Zoe took care of you, didn't she, Avie?"

Ava nodded again, a small smile appearing after her bout of tears.

Zoe pressed a tissue against her knee. "Ava, honey, I don't have a Band-Aid, but if you hold this tissue here for a minute, we may not need one, okay?"

Ava did as Zoe instructed and leaned against Caleb's chest.

Caleb looked over his daughter's head at her. "You know, when you first came into our lives, I thought I'd be the one to rescue you, but you're constantly coming to our aid."

Zoe smiled and twisted the lid back on the empty water bottle. "You don't need to rescue me. Didn't you hear Pastor Dempsey? I've already been rescued by the One who redeemed me. But I do need a friend."

"You've got that." And more. Much more. But he needed to sort out his conflicting feelings before he admitted that to anyone.

Chapter Eleven

How did a person make amends for taking someone else's life? Zoe couldn't bring Kyle back, but if she could get his parents to listen, even for a couple of minutes, maybe they'd see she was not that same person and she was truly sorry for what happened.

After spending time with Sully, the girls and Griffin at the apple orchard yesterday, Zoe wanted nothing more than to have her son on a full-time basis.

But the Jacobys' threat of custody terrified her more than anything.

They had the money and would use any means possible to discredit her and make her look unfit. She saw that first hand at her trial.

This time, she wasn't going down without a fight.

She needed to talk to them, get them to listen to reason.

She drove up the cobblestone drive, passing their small private lake and professionally landscaped acreage, and parked in front of their English Tudor home.

Her legs shook like branches in a windstorm as she rapped on the front door.

After what seemed like eternity, the door opened, and Zoe found herself face-to-face with Marcia Jacoby, who stood in the doorway drying her hands on a dish towel. She paired tan pin-striped walking shorts with a beige silk sleeveless top and tan woven sandals.

The woman's face contorted into an angry grimace. "What are you doing here?"

Zoe smoothed down the front of her red T-shirt and jeans. "Mrs. Jacoby, I just wanted to come and talk to you—"

"There's nothing you have to say that I want to hear. Now leave before I call the police and have you arrested for trespassing." She started to shut the door, but Zoe pressed her hand on the front panel, trying to stop her.

"Mrs. Jacoby, please. I just wanted to tell you how sorry I am for what happened to Kyle."

The door flew open, and Mrs. Jacoby stared at her with her jaw dropped open. Pain flickered in her eyes. "You're sorry? You think an apology will bring my son back?"

Zoe took a step back and lowered her chin. "No. I know nothing can bring back Kyle. You have to believe—"

Mrs. Jacoby clutched the doorknob and braced her other hand on the door frame. "No, Miss James, I don't have to believe a word that comes out of your mouth. Ever. You took my only child from me. Do you know how that feels?"

Even the idea caused her pulse to race. "No, not in the way you've experienced, but I'm sure I'd be devastated."

"Of course you would. As I have been for the past six years. With Kyle gone, Davis and I want to raise his son."

"Griffin is a great kid. He's innocent in all of this.

He shouldn't have to pay for what I've done. He's your grandson, after all. Do you really want to take him away from what he's always known?"

"We can give him opportunities you can't afford."

"What about what Griffin wants? He wants to live with me. I think we need to come up with an alternative solution."

"The judge will determine the best solution. Now get off my property, and don't come back. You're not welcome here." With tears glistening in her eyes, she slammed the door in Zoe's face, leaving her shaking and ready to throw up.

With wooden feet, she headed for her car. If only she could grab Griffin, drive out of town, put the past behind her and start fresh someplace else.

If only she could just keep driving.

But that was impossible.

There was one place she could go where there'd be no judgment.

Despite having left work less than an hour ago, she unlocked the back door to Canine Companions. Usually Leona and Travis minded the rescue animals, but they were still out of town, so Leona had asked if she'd go in and check on them.

She'd fed them earlier and let them play a bit before putting them back in their kennels, but they could use some extra loving and playtime.

Every time she walked into the kennel room, the sight of the dogs lying on their paws staring through the wire doors of their crates gripped her heart. She understood their needs, their longing to be free, to be loved.

Some of the dogs had been taken from cruel owners, so they were skittish or snarly, while others had been rescued as strays. Their trust in humans who promised to love them and protect them had been broken.

Thanks to Leona, though, they had opportunities to find their forever homes. If she could, Zoe would adopt each one of them and spend the rest of her life showing them how much they were worthy of being loved.

She stepped out of her red flats, leaving them by the door, and dropped her phone in one of her shoes. She filled a bucket full of disinfectant water, pulled on rubber gloves and released the latch to the first kennel.

She tried to coax Shiloh, a vanilla-colored schnauzer who had been rescued about two weeks ago, to come out so she could scrub his kennel. He whimpered and buried his face in his paws.

Zoe tugged the gloves off and extended a hand.

Shiloh's nose twitched, and he stretched out his neck to smell her scent.

Once she was confident she wouldn't spook him, she moved closer, sat down and pulled him into her lap.

The little dog quaked in her arms, but as she stroked his fur and spoke to him in soothing tones, his trembling stopped.

She rested her head against the side of his cage and cradled the dog against her chest.

Her chin quivered as tears scalded her eyes. A sob shuddered in her chest. She rubbed her cheek over the dog's fur and allowed the tears to trail down her cheeks.

Mrs. Jacoby's words scrolled through her head. Zoe's parents assured her the Jacobys had no legal grounds to gain custody of Griffin, so why were they continuing to threaten her?

With a heaviness in her chest, Zoe wiped her cheeks and set Shiloh back on his bed. She went to work scrubbing the kennels, one by one, and allowing the dogs some freedom to roam while she worked. Once she filled their food and water dishes, she closed them back into their clean kennels and tried not to let their sorrowful looks send her into another spasm of tears.

Her cell phone trilled, signaling an incoming text. She retrieved it from her shoe and opened a message from Sully.

What R U doin?

Cleaning kennels at CC. Y?

Want some help?

Almost done.

Misery loves company. Get together when UR done?

Meet me at the cabin in 30?

Sounds good. <3

She stowed her cleaning supplies and locked up.

Once she reached her cabin, she had fifteen minutes to take a quick shower and tidy up the place from Griffin spending the weekend.

With her wet hair pulled back into a ponytail and wearing a well-loved pair of jeans with a pink camp shirt, she put dishes in the sink, folded an afghan, picked up Harper's toys and wiped off the table.

Harper's ears perked up as tires crunched on the

gravel. Barking once, she raced to the screen door and jumped up to see who had arrived.

Zoe's heart picked up speed as Sully climbed out of his car. The evening sunshine glinted off his damp hair. So she wasn't the only one who had taken a shower.

Maybe hanging out with him was just what she needed tonight. Someone to make her laugh, help her forget her humiliation or the fear that shadowed her.

She slid her feet into her flip-flops and pushed through the front door as he climbed the front steps. Harper raced past her legs and bounded over to Sully. He leaned down and scratched the dog behind her ears.

She lifted a hand and gave him a small wave. "Hey."

"Hey, yourself." Shoving his hands in the front pockets of his gray shorts, he smiled and allowed his gaze to wander from her toes to her face. His orange-and-gray-striped V-neck stretched across his chest.

"I just got home. I need to walk Harper."

"I don't mind walking and talking. In fact, I've been known to do both at the same time."

"See, I knew you had exceptional abilities." Zoe stepped inside the door and traded her flip-flops for a pair of plaid canvas sneakers that offered better traction on the uneven beach.

Returning to the porch, she found Sully sitting on the front step with his arm slung around Harper, who reclined half on his lap and half on the porch. She pulled her phone from her back pocket and snapped a picture of their silhouettes shaded by the multicolored trees and the lake against the horizon. "Ready?"

Sully stood and gestured for her to lead the way.

She jogged down the steps, then whistled for Harper as she patted her leg. "Come on, Harper, let's walk."

The collie streaked past and bolted down the familiar path to the lake lined with fallen leaves of scarlet, gold and burnt orange. At the beach, Harper trotted ahead, kicking up sand.

Seagulls cawed and weaved over the water. Shades of red and orange smeared the evening sky and dripped over the darkening lake. A breeze swirled around them, whisking Zoe's ponytail into her face and ruffling Sully's hair.

Zoe bumped her shoulder against Sully's. "So, tell me what's put you in such a bad mood."

He sighed and kicked up a flat rock with the toe of his boat shoe. He picked it up and scraped off the sand with his thumb. "Today would have been my eighth wedding anniversary."

"I'm sorry. How do you feel about that?" As they walked, Zoe kept her hands in her pockets to keep from threading her fingers through his.

"Like a failure." He hurled the stone into the lake. The stone plunked into the water past the end of the dock, rippling the placid surface.

"Nice throw."

He flashed her a quick smile. "You know the night you and Griffin came over for s'mores?"

"Yes."

"I had a problem with my washer and called an old friend who had a similar problem a while back. He mentioned he had run into my ex, who is now remarried and pregnant."

"Oh, Sully."

"She walked out on us and started fresh with a new family. It's not like I'm in love with her or wish for her to come back. I just keep asking myself, why wasn't I enough?"

The anguish in his eyes mirrored what she carried in her heart. She cupped his cheek and brushed her thumb over the scruff on his jaw. "I understand, Sully. I do, but do you think maybe she's the one who felt like she couldn't measure up? Maybe she struggled with being good enough for you and the girls?"

"Hard to say." He pulled her hand down and laced his fingers through hers. "Enough about me. What happened with you today?"

With their entwined hands hanging between them, they continued along the shoreline with Harper still leading the way. "I love watching you with your girls, and the way you've been with Griffin. That means a lot to me."

"He's a great kid."

"Yeah, I know. But watching you play football with him, helping him pick apples—those things reminded me he's missing out on his own father-son relationship. I couldn't get it out of my mind. This evening, I went to Kyle's parents' house to apologize once again, to tell them how sorry I was for his death. I had hoped to reason with them about this custody thing."

"How'd that go?"

"Marcia Jacoby was as cold as the Arctic. Her hatred for me deafened her from hearing what I was trying to say. They're fighting for Griffin in revenge for what I've done. Because they lost Kyle, they want to raise his son, take him away from everything he's known. She argued they could offer him more than I can."

"Zoe…"

Zoe stopped and shaded her eyes as she looked up at him. "I get it, Sully. I do. I mean, if someone killed Griffin, I'd be devastated, too. I truly don't know how I could forgive them. She has every right to feel what she's feeling. And I hate being the cause of that, but I don't want to put Griffin through a custody battle. I can't lose him. Not again. I don't know how to fight this." Her voice thickened as her eyes burned.

Sully enfolded her in his arms. She soaked in his strength. She longed to have someone by her side to fight with her, instead of feeling like she was battling the world all on her own.

His breath warmed her cheek as he spoke. "I promise you, Zoe, I won't let them take Griffin from you. They need to prove you unfit to parent him. Besides, your parents have been doing an excellent job caring for him. A judge will see that. Maybe the Jacobys do want to raise him, but I believe they're resorting to scare tactics to break you."

Her vision blurred as her throat tightened. "It's working."

He tipped up her chin to meet her eyes. "Don't allow them to get to you."

"What do I do, Sully? What do I do?" She stepped away from him, suddenly chilled by the absence of his body heat, and threw her hands in the air.

"Trust God, Zoe. This battle belongs to Him. Allow Him to go to war on your behalf."

"I'm such a disappointment to Him. Why should He fight for me?" She blinked back the pressure building behind her eyes.

He ran the backs of his fingers over her cheek and studied her, a frown lining his forehead. His voice softened to nearly a whisper. "The question isn't why should He, but why *wouldn't* He? He loves you way more than I could ever imagine loving Ella and Ava. Your past sins disappointed Him, but nothing will separate you from

His love. Believe in that, and allow His grace to transform you into being the woman He wants you to be."

As his words saturated through the shame and self-loathing residing in her soul, she looked at him again, unable to mask what she was feeling in her heart. "We're both searching for second chances, looking for our own fresh starts. I'm so glad you came back into my life."

An expression she'd seen him use so many times with his daughters—a mixture of amazement and joy—crossed his face. "I like to think our meeting again was no accident, but a part of God's bigger picture for both of us."

"I really needed a friend like you." She rested her cheek against his chest, the softness of his shirt caressing her skin. Listening to the pounding of his heart, she savored the lingering scent of his body wash, a mixture of ocean breezes and sunshine.

If only she could stay wrapped in his arms, sheltered from the harsh realities of life.

"Just a friend?"

She drew back and peered into his eyes, leafy green under a sunburst of gold. Her lungs stalled as she pondered his question, almost afraid to guess what implication hung between them.

A slight smile tugging at his mouth, Sully trailed his finger over her cheekbone, the outline of her lips, then down the hollow of her neck. He tugged her hair free from its ponytail holder and finger-combed it to fall around her shoulders. He cradled her face as her arms slid around his waist.

Anticipation swirled in the valley of her soul. A sigh whispered past her parted lips. Sully lowered his mouth and brushed a featherlight kiss across her lips. His arms slid around her as he claimed her lips again, this time erasing any doubts from her mind about their future relationship.

She'd finally found someone who truly understood her and showered her with compassion in spite of her past sins. Did she dare to risk hope that it could be part of God's divine plan for them?

Holding Zoe in his arms felt so right. Even though they'd reconnected only a short time ago, Caleb couldn't ignore what his heart was telling him.

He was in love with Zoe James.

Again.

And yes, that scared him just a little. Having been burned once, he wanted to make completely sure she felt the same way. He didn't doubt their shared values, but he needed to know he was making the right choice for his family.

At least this time he wasn't competing with someone else's affections.

He enveloped her against his chest and rested his cheek on the top of her head, breathing in the fragrance of her shampoo. As the waves lapped at the shore and the sun melted against the water, a sensation he hadn't felt in a long time flowed over him, filling in the gaps and gashes in his heart flayed open at his ex-wife's betrayal.

Zoe wasn't anything like Val.

The more he spent time with her, the more he saw the girl he'd loved back in college. Life had changed both of them, but her sweet spirit remained the same. With time, she could put the past behind her and embrace the future God longed to give her.

Hopefully with him by her side.

Zoe pulled back and looked up at him. "You're quiet."

"Just thinking."

"About what?"

"You. Me. The future."

"Do you ever wish you could see into the future?"

"I don't know. Maybe sometimes. But if we could see the future, then we wouldn't really need to rely on God."

"True. Sometimes it's easier just knowing things are going to work out." Worry colored her eyes as she turned in his arms and rested her back against him to look at the lake.

He wrapped his arms around her and gave her a gentle squeeze. "I know it's hard, Zoe. If I were in your shoes, I'd hate the uncertainty, too."

"If you were in my shoes, you'd stretch them out." She glanced at him with a smile on her face.

He laughed. "Yes, I would. After I was shot and Val left, I didn't think I'd be able to handle two little girls. We definitely have our moments, but they're clean, fed and well loved."

"You're a great dad, Sully."

"And you're a wonderful mom. Griffin knows that."

"I just hope I get the opportunity to show him."

"You're doing that now."

"What do you say we head back to the cabin?"

"Sounds like a plan to me." Caleb reached for her hand, and they trudged across the sand to the path that led through the woods.

Caleb's phone rang as soon as they reached the cabin steps. He fished it out of his pocket and read Sarah's number on his screen. He answered. "Hey, sis. What's up?"

"Caleb. Mom called."

"Yeah? What's going on?"

"Dad had a heart attack." Her voice shook.

"What? When? How is he?" His eyes darted to Zoe, who watched him with concern.

"About three hours ago. Apparently he collapsed at the office, and someone called 911. He's been airlifted to Pittsburgh. Mom wants to go down, but I don't feel she should go alone."

"No, she shouldn't. We can pick her up on the way down."

"What about the girls?"

Caleb sighed and rubbed his thumb and forefinger across his eyes. "I guess I'll have to stay put. Can you handle taking Mom?"

"Yes, I'll manage."

"Okay, I'll head back and we'll go from there."

"See you soon."

Caleb ended the call, pressed his arm against one of the support beams on the porch and braced his head in the crook of his elbow.

Zoe touched his shoulder. "Sully, what's wrong?"

"Sarah called. My dad's had a heart attack." He shared the details his sister had given him. "I'm sorry, but I need to go."

She waved away his apology. "Of course. Is there anything I can do?"

"Conjure up a nanny for me? Because of the girls, I'm going to stay put while Sarah and Mom go to the hospital."

"I may not be named Mary Poppins, but I'll stay with the girls, if you'd like."

He shook his head. "I can't ask you to do that."

"You didn't. I offered."

"What about work?"

"Leona will be back tomorrow. I'll call her and explain the situation. I know she won't have a problem with it."

He tucked a strand of hair behind her ear. "Zoe, you are a lifesaver. Sarah can handle Mom, but I feel I should be there, too."

She covered his hand with her own. "He's your dad. Of course you should. You head home, and I'll meet you there after I grab a few things. Do you mind if Harper comes?"

"No, of course not. As long as you don't mind throwing caring for Riley into the mix."

"Of course not. I love the little guy." She turned and headed up the steps. "I'll throw a bag together and meet you at your house."

Caleb reached out and grabbed her wrist. With a gentle tug, he pulled her to him. He gathered her in his arms and kissed her.

"You are amazing." He released her and headed for his car, savoring the sweetness of their kiss as he crawled behind the wheel and started the engine.

Chapter Twelve

The girls should've been in bed ages ago, but Zoe had a tough time enforcing it after the fun day they had playing dress up, hosting a tea party and polishing off bath time with polka-dotted pedicures.

She added the last purple dot to Ava's tiny toe, and then blew across her foot. "Okay, sweetie, let those dry. You like?"

Ava looked at her toenails, then at Zoe and nodded with a small smile on her lips.

Zoe brushed her damp hair behind her ear, releasing the scent of her baby shampoo.

Ella crawled onto the couch with a book in her hand. "Zoe, will you read me a story?"

"Sure, sweetie." Zoe situated Ava on her lap, then reached for the storybook Ella had chosen—*No Matter What*, a story about a little fox who questions if his mommy truly loves him.

Ella snuggled in next to her. Zoe wrapped her arms around both girls and opened the book.

She read using two different voices, eliciting giggles

from both girls. She hadn't read a children's book since Griffin was a toddler, before her life fell apart.

She finished the story to find Ava fighting to keep her eyes open. Zoe brushed a kiss across her forehead. "Hey, little one, how about if we head to bed?"

Ella held the book open in her lap to the page of the little fox lying in bed next to his mother. She rubbed her finger across Mama Fox's nose.

She looked up at Zoe with questioning eyes. "Zoe?"

Zoe brushed her hair off her forehead. "Yes, honey?"

"My mommy is far away. Does she still love us?"

"Oh, baby." Zoe lifted Ella onto her lap and pressed her head against her chest. She didn't want to lie to the child, but what could she say? "Ella, I'm sure your mommy loves you very much. Remember the story— love surrounds us wherever we are."

"If she loved us, why did she leave us and make Daddy so sad?"

"I don't know, sweetie. I do know your daddy loves you very much, and you make him so happy." Ava's gentle snores warmed Zoe's neck. "You need to get into bed."

Zoe stood and held out her hand. Ella looked at the cover of the book once more, then set it on the couch. She took Zoe's hand, and they walked down the hall to the girls' room. Zoe pulled back the covers and laid Ava on her bed. She pulled the covers up to her chin and kissed her petal-soft cheek.

Zoe turned to find Ella had climbed into bed already. She smoothed the covers over the child and caressed her cheek. "Thanks for the fun day, sweet girl."

Ella reached for Zoe's hand and pressed a kiss onto her palm. "I liked it."

Smiling at her, Zoe brushed her fingers across the child's cheek. "Good night, Ella."

Ella reached for her hand. "I love you, Zoe."

"I love you, too, Ella. Very much." With tears pressing against the backs of her eyes, she headed for the door and flicked off the light. For a moment, though, she stood in the darkness with only the soft glow of the night-light casting shadows across the floor.

How could Valerie leave behind those two adorable little girls? Didn't she realize what precious treasures she'd had?

While Ella was in school, Zoe had taken Ava to see the rescued puppies. She had seemed particularly taken with Shiloh—the one Zoe cuddled with yesterday.

She moved into the living room and gathered the nail polish bottles, the storybook and the girls' art supplies they used to draw pictures for Sully.

A gentle quiet drifted over the room, but Zoe didn't feel peace. She sighed and sat on the couch. Harper settled at her feet while Riley jumped into her lap.

She picked up a framed photo of Sully and the girls. She ran her fingers over their smiles. Ella may be questioning her mother's love, but no one could accuse Sully of not loving his daughters. He didn't just say it, he showed it in everything he did. A father's relationship with his daughters needed to be protected and cherished.

Spending the day with the girls in their home stirred a longing in Zoe. When Mom had dropped Griffin off this afternoon for a couple of hours, the house had seemed almost complete. Of course, Sully being away created a hole felt by everyone, even Riley.

She could see herself living in the three-bedroom ranch home with the sturdy oak shading the deck and large backyard and being a part of this family. She'd make sure the girls never doubted they were loved.

What if Sully had chosen her over a decade ago?

Her life would have turned out differently. But she wouldn't have Griffin, and she wouldn't trade him for anything.

Zoe set the photo back on the table and pulled her phone out of her back pocket. She thumbed through the texts she and Sully had been sending back and forth. He ended every one the same—with "<3," the text symbol for a heart.

The time they'd spent together as trainer and client reminded her of the guy she used to know. Then, after Riley and the girls had progressed to where they didn't need Zoe's services, she allowed herself to consider the possibility of a relationship with Sully and his daughters that moved beyond the bounds of professionalism and friendship. She wanted to take things slow for everyone's sake.

No matter how much she tried to fight it, she could no longer deny what her heart was saying—she was in love with Caleb Sullivan. And she had no idea what to do about it.

From the moment Caleb dropped Sarah and his mother off at his parents' house, all he could think about was climbing into bed and sleeping until noon.

With the girls, he'd be happy with at least five hours of solid sleep. Now that his father was stable, the doctors encouraged them to go home and get some rest. Sarah and his mom planned to go back to the hospital tomorrow, but he needed to be there for the girls. He couldn't be away from them for long stretches at a time.

Every time he left, Ella asked if he was coming back. Even on the phone that evening, he'd promised he'd be home tonight. She'd see him when she woke up in the morning.

As he turned onto his street, his front porch light shined like a beacon against the midnight sky, filling him with warmth knowing someone was waiting for him. He longed for that to become permanent.

Once he parked the car in the attached garage, he headed into the kitchen through the side door. The scent of lemon cleaner lingered in the air.

Zoe stood at the sink with her back to him as she hummed and swayed to the music playing in her ears. A cord led from her back pocket to her ears, which explained why she didn't turn when he entered.

He walked up behind her, slid his arms around her waist and lowered his lips to her ear. "Hi, honey. I'm home."

She gasped and swiveled in his arms. Seeing him, a smile spread across her face. She gripped his upper arms. "Hey, you."

Loose strands of hair escaped her clip and framed her face. Water splattered her Shelby Lake Lions sweatshirt. He breathed in the sweet fragrance beckoning him to come closer.

All too happy to oblige, Caleb lowered his head and kissed her. "Hi, yourself."

Without releasing her, he turned so his back was against the sink and she wouldn't feel pinned. "I missed you."

Her arms curled around his neck. "I missed you, too. How's your dad?"

"He's stable. They did an EKG and ended up putting

in a stent. They'll monitor him over the next seventy-two hours. If anything happens, it's usually in that time frame."

"Glad to hear he's better. How's your mom?"

"She's tired. Sarah is staying with her tonight. They'll go back tomorrow."

"Sully, if you want to go back, I can stay with the girls again."

"You've done so much already, Zoe. Besides, I can't stay away from the girls for that long. How were they? I hope they didn't give you too much of a hard time."

"Are you kidding? They're adorable." She shared how they spent the day and concluded with Ella's questions after she read the story.

Caleb sighed and rubbed a thumb and forefinger over his eyes. "I know they miss their mom. It's tough trying to be both mom and dad to them. What if I screw up? What if I miss something important?"

"Sully, you pay attention to the details. When we were at Bartlett, you kept me from failing algebra."

"I was paid to be your tutor."

"Maybe so, but you went the extra mile putting it into terms I'd understand. You never forgot my favorite ice cream flavor. You remembered my birthday when Kyle forgot. You walked me across campus after my night class. You drove me all the way back to Shelby Lake when my battery died just before spring break. Cut yourself some slack." She cupped his cheek. "It's okay to miss the little things from time to time as long as you remember the big stuff. You see me like no one else does, Sully, and to me, that's huge. You're a good man. Never doubt that."

Her words soaked in and patched up the worn-out, torn

pieces of his heart that had been gashed open by his own unwillingness to forgive himself for keeping his family from falling apart.

He reached for her hand and squeezed. "Thank you, Zoe. You have no idea how much that means to me. Do you mind if we go into the living room? I'm beat."

"No, not at all. Can I get you anything?"

"You don't need to take care of me." He reached for her hand as they headed for the couch.

When he'd left this morning, a basket of the girls' clothes had been sitting on the chair. Their dolls littered the floor. A sheen of dust and dog hair lay on the table.

The basket was missing, toys had been cleaned up, the table dusted and marks in the carpet showed the vacuum had been run.

"Zoe, you didn't need to clean my house."

"I love to clean, so it was no problem. Besides, the girls helped, and we had fun doing it." She handed him a folded paper and a stack of envelopes. "The girls colored you a picture. Here's your mail, too. I don't know where you usually keep it."

"Thank you." He opened the white paper to find Ava's blobby shapes and Ella's stick people. Neat lettering— Zoe's obviously—above the people noted them as Daddy, Avie and Ella. Off to the side, a little blob had Riley written above it. He grinned. "A family portrait."

Zoe peered over his shoulder. "I do see the resemblance."

He set the picture on the table and leafed through the pile of mail, separating bills from junk. A manila envelope with no return address lay at the bottom of the stack.

He slid a finger under the seal and tore it open. He

pulled out a couple of photos and a short note. It read: "What do you think of your 'friend' now?"

Caleb frowned, then flipped over the photos, leafing through them quickly. His heart ratcheted against his ribs.

No.

No way.

The photos showed Zoe standing outside a dive bar, hanging on to another woman, who appeared three sheets to the wind. He squinted and pulled the photos closer to his face. Was that a beer bottle in her hand?

Ice sluiced through his veins.

He braced his elbow on his knee and dug the heel of his hand into his forehead. He was an idiot. A fool. Why did he think people could change?

Zoe touched his shoulder. "Hey, are you okay? You've gone white."

He stiffened and dropped his hand to look at her. Genuine concern marked her face. He tossed the pictures in her lap and slumped against the back of the couch. "You tell me?"

She pictured up the photos, sucked in a breath and pressed a hand against her mouth. "Where did you get these?"

"Is that you?"

"Yes, but—"

"No buts, Zoe. I truly thought you were different."

"I am different, Sully, but I was there for a reason."

"Of course you were. Between my years on the force and being married to an alcoholic, I've heard all of the excuses, the reasons, the lies. I'm not stupid." He jumped to his feet and paced in front of the couch. "Or maybe I am. I let my guard down and fell in love with you all over again."

"You love me?"

"Like I said, I'm an idiot. I've had a long day. If you don't mind…"

She shook her head, tears glimmering in her eyes. "Wait a minute. Don't I get a say in this? A chance to explain? I never want to do anything to hurt you or the girls."

"Too late for that." An ache pulsed in the pit of his stomach.

"I'm sorry for what your ex-wife did to you, but you need to realize I'm not like her." Zoe picked up her purse off the table and slid the strap over her shoulder. "Things aren't what they seem, Sully."

"Apparently not."

A tear trailed down her cheek as she pressed her palm to her heart. She gave him a sad smile. "If you can't trust me and believe a picture over the past weeks we've shared, then I guess I'm not the right person for you after all. Goodbye, Caleb."

The door closed behind her with a whispered click. Caleb shoved his hands into his pockets and forced himself not to run after her. What if he'd made a mistake?

No.

He had to stand his ground. He had his daughters to protect. They'd went through enough with their mother's addiction and abandonment. He wasn't going to subject them to that lifestyle all over again. Or himself. He couldn't take it again. He was finally regaining some sense of stability.

So why did it feel as if his heart had been dragged down the street behind Zoe's car?

Chapter Thirteen

No matter how hard she ran or how many times she tried to erase it from her memory, Zoe couldn't forget the look on Sully's face when he tossed those photos onto her lap.

For a fleeting moment, his eyes showed what others had said time and time again—redemption wasn't meant for someone like her.

The early morning breeze cooled her heated cheeks as she ran along the path winding around the lake. She tightened the leash around her right hand and looked at Harper running alongside her. "Let's do one more lap, girl."

Harper panted in reply and maintained a similar pace.

Zoe's feet ate up the dirt path in measured strides. Her lungs burned as her joints and muscles heated. An ache under her ribs caused her feet to slow. Her chest heaved as her limbs, fueled by adrenaline, trembled—from her workout or her self-loathing, she wasn't quite sure.

How long did it take for broken hearts to heal? Or even for the pain to diminish a little?

Hers was going to take an eternity.

Somehow Zoe would manage to keep the pieces intact. She'd done it before, and she'd do it again.

Once Sully no longer needed her dog-training services, she should have dropped contact, but she continued to gravitate to him like a moth to a flame. Like that moth, she ended up getting burned.

Her eyes burned from getting only three hours of sleep after she left Sully's. Her head throbbed from her crying jag. The three cups of coffee she had downed to feel somewhat human curdled in her stomach.

She pulled off her James & Son Insurance baseball hat, rubbed the seam of her running shirt over her forehead, then readjusted the hat on her head, pulling her ponytail through the back loop. She slipped her sunglasses onto her face, paused to retie her shoe, then guided Harper back home.

She needed to get ready for work.

Her feet slowed as the cabin came into view.

Leona sat in her great-grandfather's rocking chair with her feet up on the railing and sipped from a Cuppa Josie's to-go cup.

Zoe bent and grabbed her knees to catch her breath. She swallowed her fatigue and climbed the steps, forcing a smile onto her face. "Hey, Leona. What's up?"

Leona pointed to the twin to-go cup sitting on the small table between the rockers. "Want a cup?"

Her stomach chugged at the thought. Zoe held up a hand and shook her head. "I've had three already."

"Three? Girl, you're going to be buzzing."

That was the point, stay busy so she didn't have time to think, time to dwell on the look that'd crossed Caleb's face when he'd asked her to leave. Or the way his "I love you" echoed inside her head. Or the way her heart shattered on the floor of her chest in a billion shards.

Leona cocked her head and searched Zoe's face. "You okay?"

"I will be." Fresh tears pricked the backs of her eyes. If she said anything else, she'd be crying on Leona's shoulder. She didn't want to deal with another headache.

Leona leaned forward and patted the other chair. "Have a seat and tell Leona what's going on."

She couldn't talk. Not when the wounds were still fresh.

"Shouldn't we be getting to work?"

"Travis is there. He can handle the fur kids for a few minutes. I wanted to talk to you about something."

"Couldn't this have waited until I got to work?"

"I have a lot of catching up to do once I get to the office, so I wanted to stop by before I got my nose buried in paperwork. This way I can talk to you without distraction."

Zoe settled into the rocker and rested her head against the frame. "How's your mom?"

"She's better and recuperating at the nursing home near their house. Dad needs the rest." Leona tucked her feet under her thighs and reached for her coffee. "You know, Zoe, I can't thank you enough for all you've done around here while I spent so much time at the hospital with Mom."

"No thanks needed. Your family needed you. It was the least I could do. After all, you offered me a second chance when no one else would."

"We serve a God of second chances."

"I'm sorry about costing you a family from the Kids & Canines training class."

Leona waved away her apology. "Good riddance, I

say. If they can't show grace and respect toward my best girl, then I don't need their business."

Zoe straightened. "Leona, you can't afford to turn away business because of me."

"Sure I can. Zoe, listen to me. You have amazing skills, and it's about time people started seeing and benefitting from them." Leona reached down to her side and pulled a sheaf of papers out of the bag by her feet. She pulled off the binder clip. "While I was at my parents', I emailed a letter of apology with a discount coupon for a future class. I also expressed my thanks for your willingness to step in at the last minute. I asked the parents to fill out an evaluation form."

Leona leafed through the papers. "Here are a few comments. 'Zoe showed patience and skill with our dog and with our daughter.' Here's another. 'Zoe's approach helped my son get our dog to sit after only one lesson, strengthening his confidence.' Here's one of my favorites. 'Zoe's charm and one-on-one training helped my daughter overcome her fear of our dog.'"

Leona dropped the papers into her bag and turned to Zoe, smiling. "I'm so proud of the work you're doing here, Zoe."

"Thank you, Leona."

"No, thank you, Zoe. You're the most talented dog handler I've seen in years."

Like a withered plant thirsting for water, her battered spirit was showered by Leona's words, soaking her with hope. She smiled, but didn't move, almost afraid that if she did, then the feeling would disappear.

Now if only she could stop aching for Sully.

Zoe stood and leaned against the railing. "Thanks for letting me know, Leona. I appreciate it."

"I want you to take the rest of the week off, paid. It's the least I could do for all you've done."

Three days off? What would she do besides spending it moping about Sully?

"That's very generous, but I'd prefer to work. Seriously."

"Girl, you are seriously dedicated."

More like stupid. Stupid to fall in love with a guy who painted her with his ex's brush.

Tires crunched on the gravel. Zoe leaned back to see who was coming and spied a black sedan.

Sully.

What was he doing here?

Her heart picked up speed, but she forced herself to remain calm.

Seconds later, he rounded the side of the cabin with his head down and hands shoved in his pockets. He did a double take when he saw her on the front porch.

He wore jeans with a rip in the right knee and a flannel shirt over a navy T-shirt. Circles shadowed his eyes. Lines etched his forehead and around his mouth. At least she wasn't the only one who looked like death.

Leona stood and gathered her bag and cup, her eyes zipping between the two of them. "Well, I need to get to work. Think about what I said, Zoe. Take advantage of the downtime."

Zoe gave her a quick hug. "Thanks, friend."

As soon as Leona walked to her car and backed out of the parking space, Zoe squared her shoulders and faced Sully, her insides a trembling mess. "You're the last person I expected to see this morning."

He pressed one foot against the edge of the bottom step and rubbed a hand over his face. "Yeah, well, I tossed and turned all night. I acted like a jerk last night and wanted to apologize. I was stressed-out from being at that hospital with my dad, and then those pictures…"

She crossed her arms over her chest and glared at him. A coil of hurt unfurled in her stomach. "You made assumptions and wouldn't let me explain."

He met her glare with a steady gaze. "In my line of work—and after being married to an alcoholic—I've heard more excuses and explanations than you could possibly imagine. So I guess I've become a bit cynical."

"Ya think?"

He threw his hands in the air. "I don't know what else to say, Zoe."

"How about believing in me? You were so quick to defend me before, but now you have doubts?" Tears simmered behind her eyes, but she wasn't about to let him see her cry. A slow burn simmered in her veins. Her heart throbbed. "I am not your ex-wife. I've been working hard to overcome my past."

"I'm sorry."

"My friend Gina called and asked me to meet her at The Sassy Cat. I couldn't violate my sentencing agreement, so I parked in the lot next to The Sassy Cat. I never entered the bar, nor did I step foot on the property."

"But the pictures—"

"Forget those pictures, Sully. I'm telling you I wasn't inside that bar. I never had a drink. That bottle was Gina's. I took it from her and grabbed her to keep her from face-planting on the pavement."

"I'm such an idiot."

"About this—yes, you are. I know you're stressed about your dad. I can forgive that, but you didn't even give me a chance to explain. I thought you of all people believed in me, Sully."

"I do, Zoe. I do. But those photos were pretty incriminating."

"They definitely did their job, didn't they?" She didn't even try to ease the threads of sarcasm that tightened around her words.

"I screwed up. I hope that doesn't change things between us."

Was he serious?

"Of course it changes things." She tossed her hands up and paced the length of the porch, her voice growing louder and words coming faster as she moved. "It's apparent you don't trust me. At least not about this. You're just waiting for me to go back to that old life. You're expecting me to be like Val and choose the bottle over you."

"No, Zoe. It's not like that." He jogged up the steps and reached out to touch her.

She jerked away. "Don't touch me. Yes, it is, Sully. I truly thought we were going somewhere. I was beginning to see a future for us. Now *I'm* the one who was the idiot." This time she didn't try to hold back the tears that slid down her cheeks.

Tires crunched on the gravel driveway.

She went weeks without visitors, and now she had at least three in one day.

Two doors slammed. A pair of uniformed Shelby Lake police officers rounded the corner of the cabin.

Her limbs trembled. Pressure built up behind her breastbone as her heart picked up speed.

What were they doing there?

Zoe recognized one of them as the same one who delivered the custody petition to her parents. Officer Reynolds. And the other was Sully's neighbor who confronted him at the go-kart track. Turner.

Sully stepped in front of her. "Guys, what's going on?"

"Step aside, Sullivan." Officer Turner elbowed past him and withdrew cuffs from his utility belt. "Miss James, you're under arrest. You have the right to remain silent…"

She tuned out the rest of the officer's Miranda warning as he slipped the handcuffs on her wrists, the shackled metal spiraling her back in time. But, unlike the last time she was arrested, this time she was innocent. Her eyes darted from the officer to Sully, who watched with sorrowful eyes.

"But I didn't do anything."

Why wouldn't anyone believe her?

The Jacobys finally figured out how to get their revenge. She couldn't go back to jail, but there was no way she could prove she was innocent. Gina had been too drunk to remember anything, so it was Zoe's word against everyone else's.

As the officer tucked her into the back of the patrol car, she shifted a glance to Sully.

The despair he wore cinched what she'd realized upon waking that morning—there was no hope for a future with him.

Caleb stared into his cooling cup of coffee, still trying to make sense of what had happened this morning.

Seeing Zoe in handcuffs caused his stomach to churn. There was nothing he could do about it.

Was she as innocent as she claimed?

After leaving the cabin, he had driven to The Sassy Cat and parked in the lot next to the bar. From what Zoe said, it was possible for her to be close by and help her friend without actually stepping foot on the other property.

So why was he so quick to accuse her?

Didn't matter now. She wanted nothing to do with him. The future he imagined with her evaporated like the morning mist over the lake.

The door to the suite in the family house across the street from the hospital opened, and his sister walked in carrying fast-food bags. The scent of grilled burgers and French fries singed his nose.

Sarah had come back to his place early that morning to grab some clothes. She offered to keep the girls while he went and apologized to Zoe. When he returned, she convinced him to pack up the girls and bring them to the family house. Seeing the smile on Mom's tired face wiped away any indecision he may have had about pulling Ella out of school for a couple of days. Mom and Sarah promised to help take care of them. Between the three of them, they could take shifts sitting with Dad and entertaining the girls.

Dad remained in the cardiac unit to monitor his heart activity after the stent had been placed. Too bad there wasn't a fix for Griffin's broken heart.

Sarah laid a hand on his shoulder. "Why are you looking so mopey? Dad's going to be fine. The doctors are pleased with the outcome of the procedure. The next seventy-two hours are just monitoring his heart activity."

Caleb dragged a hand over his face and set his coffee on the side table. "I have no doubt about Dad. He's too stubborn to let something like a heart attack slow him down."

"Then what's wrong?"

He hadn't told Sarah what happened this morning. Instead he had hurried to gather clothes and toys for the girls, hoping by keeping busy he wouldn't feel the guilt gnawing him from the inside out.

Caleb pushed to his feet and walked to the front window overlooking the street. He shoved his hands into his pockets and watched the traffic. People entered and exited the hospital. A jackhammer pounded up chunks of asphalt as a road crew redirected the road patterns so they could fix the street.

He blew out a breath, then turned to his sister who joined him at the window. "You were right, Sarah. Just try to hold back your gloating."

"What was I right about?"

"Zoe." He told her about the pictures, his accusations, his attempt at an apology and then Zoe's arrest.

"Caleb, I'd never gloat about anything like that. I'm so sorry you're hurting."

"I feel so helpless."

"What happened wasn't your fault. Besides, you need to protect the girls."

"Zoe would never hurt them."

"How do you know?"

"Because she's not like that. She loves them. She takes care of animals. She helps her family at Agape House. She teaches little girls how to get dogs to sit. She reads her Bible on the porch in the rain." The more he talked, the more a pain gripped his chest.

"Then why did you freak out about the pictures if you believe that?"

"Because I'm an idiot. I was stressed-out about Dad and tired from the drive. And, yes, I've had some reservations, but they're more about what others would think or say, not about how I feel about her."

"Why are you telling me and not her?"

"There's this little thing called family. You may have heard of it?"

She shoved her elbow in his ribs and smiled. "Jerk. Seriously, though, our family won't fall apart if you leave for a while to talk to Zoe. Mom and I will take care of the girls."

"You've done enough, don't you think?"

"Dude, that's what family's all about. Just let us help. I'm sure the time will come when you can pay me back, but for now, go fix that girl's broken heart."

Caleb shoved his hands in his pockets. "What if she doesn't want to see me? What if it's too late?"

"You're not a quitter, so don't give up now. If she's truly the one, then fight for her. Prove you believe in her."

He looked out the window and reflected on what his sister just said. Other than using his words to convince her, he wasn't sure what else to do or say.

His eyes drifted over the street. Something caught his attention. He squinted, and then a smile spread across his face. He turned to Sarah. "I know how to prove Zoe's innocent."

She raised an eyebrow. "Other than just taking her word for it?"

"This will prove it to the judge." He pointed out the window. "There's a security camera on that pole. I know there's one facing the parking lot Zoe was in. I saw it earlier, but it didn't register until now."

"Good. Now get out of here and go play hero. You have a lot of sweet talking to do."

After talking with the girls about where he was going

and promising to come back, Caleb headed for his car. Zoe was definitely worth fighting for. Now he'd convince her *they* were worth fighting for, too.

Chapter Fourteen

Dressed in flannel pants and a long-sleeved T-shirt after her shower, Zoe padded downstairs with Harper at her heels, hoping she'd never have to feel a prison uniform against her skin again or hear the clank of cell door being closed, trapping her within its restrictive confines.

Unfortunately her days in the courtroom weren't over. After she had been arrested and booked, she spent the night in temporary holding. Thankfully she had been one of the first to go before the judge this morning.

She had called her parents yesterday before being escorted to her cell. Seeing them in the courtroom this morning filled her with shame at having to put them through the same business again. Dad must have called his attorney, because Ralph Emerson appealed on her behalf. The judge set her bail, which Dad thankfully paid. Otherwise, she'd have to stay locked up since she hadn't saved up enough yet. She hated being more indebted to him, but what choice did she have? Now she had to wait for her arraignment hearing.

In the meantime, she was determined to bind up her broken heart and put one foot in front of the other to show the judge today she was innocent of the accusations. First, she needed an infusion of caffeine.

She started the coffee, and while it brewed, she took Harper outside and grabbed the morning paper. With no internet or cable at the cabin, the paper allowed her a glimpse of what was happening in the community and around the world.

Zoe poured a cup of coffee into her favorite mug, added a splash of milk and carried it to her favorite corner of the couch.

She unfolded the paper and took a sip as she smoothed out the front page. It read: "Agape House—Convict Rehabilitation or Ruin?"

Zoe jerked up, sloshing coffee on her thigh. Her heart hammered as her throat threatened to close. She slammed her coffee on the table. Ignoring the spilled coffee on her leg, she gripped the newspaper with two hands.

A grainy black-and-white photo of Zoe and Gina in The Sassy Cat's parking lot was shown under the bold headline. Another photo showed Gina being taken out of her trailer on a stretcher.

The article stated the background of Agape House— how her family had worked with the community to have it open before her release. Then the article went on to give details about her arrest and conviction four years ago, including a picture of her in handcuffs.

The article questioned whether Agape House was truly a benefit to society, or if it was offering ex-convicts a stepping stone back into their former lives.

Heat infused her face chased by a clamminess that slicked her skin. Her blood boiled.

This article wasn't responsible reporting with its misleading information and half-truths. The only solid facts were that Agape House was founded by her family before her release and her conviction charge. Everything else was conjecture and lies by a "reliable source" close to the family.

Whose family? Not hers, that's for sure.

Tabloid journalism.

Didn't the *Shelby Lake Gazette* hold itself to a higher standard? What was that editor thinking by approving this article?

But headlines sold, and this one was a doozy.

Davis Jacoby had to be behind this.

Her attempt to help her friend had combusted. Zoe worked her tail off to become the kind of person who could hold her head up with pride, but all she managed to accomplish was bringing more shame to her family.

What was going to happen to Griffin when he heard about this? He didn't ask for any of this, yet he had to deal with the rumors and whispers.

Not to mention her parents, her dad's insurance business, Ian and Agnes. All of them would be the subjects of town gossip and tainted because she'd tried to help a friend. And Sully would read the article, and it would only reaffirm his suspicions all over again.

Her chest tightened. Her breathing came out in irregular gasps. The feeling like she was falling swirled through her head, making her feel woozy. She tossed the paper on the cushion and dropped her head between her knees.

Sully said she needed to stop running and stand up for herself, but he didn't get it. Staying here created problems for those she loved.

She needed to leave this town and not look back. Make a fresh start where no one knew her name.

But where would she go?

Didn't matter. Any place had to be better than here.

But what about Griffin? Her parents? Ian and Agnes? Sully and the girls?

She'd miss them all terribly, especially Griffin. With very little money and no destination in mind, she couldn't take him with her. Besides, he'd been doing so well in her parents' care. He'd be better off without her.

If she was going, then she needed to pack, then swing by Canine Companions and let Leona know she wouldn't be coming back to work. She regretted not being able to give her boss two weeks' notice, but hopefully she would understand and provide her with a reference at a later date.

Zoe pushed to her feet. Once the room stopped spinning, she hurried up the steps with Harper at her heels. After changing into jeans, a long-sleeved T-shirt and warm socks, she ran a brush through her hair and pulled it into a ponytail.

She pulled out her first drawer, grabbed an armful of shirts, then searched her room for something to put them in.

When she moved in, she had used her parents' suitcases, but those had been returned. Her packing boxes had been dropped at the recycling center.

Grocery and trash bags would have to do, which meant a trip to the kitchen. With her arms full, she hurried downstairs, dumped the clothes on the couch and headed for the kitchen to find the bags. Packing would be easier downstairs.

She headed back upstairs and made several trips back to the living room. She retrieved her toiletries, then checked her room a final time. Hangers swung in her empty closet.

Empty.

That's about how she felt.

She returned to the couch and started shoving clothes into black bags. While upstairs she should have grabbed a couple of blankets, especially since she'd probably have to sleep in her car for a couple of days until she found a cheap room to rent.

Jumping up, she raced for the stairs. Her foot caught on the bag she'd been filling. She stumbled and managed to catch herself from falling, but her jaw caught the corner of the coffee table.

Her teeth clamped her bottom lip. Pain shot through her jaw as the metallic taste of blood flavored her mouth. She dropped to the floor, cradling her face.

Her chest constricted as tears scalded her eyes. Her breath came out in gasps. She buried her face in her hands and sobbed.

Caleb knocked on the cabin door. Harper barked inside, but Zoe didn't come to the door. Her car was parked in the driveway. He rapped his knuckles again, but instead of waiting, he cracked open the door and peeked inside. "Zoe? You here?"

Clothes littered her living room, as if they had been strewn in a hurry. Was she going somewhere? Looking for something?

Harper barked and bounded down the steps. She greeted Caleb at the door. "Hey, Harper. Where's Zoe?"

A moment later, Zoe walked barefoot down the stairs. She entered the living room with a pink washcloth pressed to her face. She wore jeans and a long-sleeved

T-shirt. Her hair had been pulled into a ponytail. "What are you doing here?"

Ignoring her snappy tone, Sully straightened from petting Harper. He frowned as his eyes roamed her face, taking in the crimson welt on her chin and bloody, swollen bottom lip. He gently touched her cheek. "What happened? Are you okay?"

"Do I look okay?" Glaring, Zoe pushed past him and headed for the kitchen. She reached for a bottle of pain reliever by the sink and downed two tablets with some water.

He followed her and leaned against the kitchen counter. "No, not really. You look like a mess, actually."

Zoe scoffed, tears shimmering in her eyes. "Thanks, just what every girl wants to hear." She pushed past him and returned to the living room.

He didn't mean to make her cry. This wasn't how he had things mapped out in his head.

Caleb waved a hand over the living room. "Laundry day? Or cleaning out your closets?"

"Neither."

"What happened, Zoe? And why are your clothes all over the living room?"

"I tripped over a bag and banged my chin on the coffee table. I put my top teeth through the inside of my bottom lip."

He touched her shoulder and turned her so he could survey her face again. "Ouch. Maybe you should get that checked out."

She dragged a hand through her hair. "I'm not going anywhere. I'm trapped here."

"What's going on?" He reached for her, but she pushed past him and stomped to the table where this morning's paper lay scattered. She snatched it up, crinkling it in her fist. "Did you read this?"

"Yes."

"I've ruined everything, Sully." A tear rolled down the side of her nose. She dashed it away. "It's a bunch of lies. Now the community will try to shut down Agape House all because I tried to help a friend. And my family won't ever let me have my son back."

"Zoe, the right people will know the truth."

"Like you? You didn't believe me, so how can I expect strangers to believe me?"

She flung her arm, pointing past the cabin door. "The fine residents of Shelby Lake will read that drivel and think the worst."

"Then let them." A muscle jumped in the side of Caleb's jaw. Pressing his back against the counter, he crossed his arms and ankles and shrugged. "The article's false, Zoe. Agape House can stand on its own feet. You can, too. You're strong. You can't control what people think and say. You can only control how you react to them."

"How could you say that? You took one look at those pictures and jumped to conclusions without listening to me. What makes you think anyone else will be any different? Without this community's support, Agape House ceases to exist. And what about my son? He's too young to understand what's happening."

"This will blow over in a day or two, and everyone will be just fine."

"That's easy for you to say. This doesn't affect you." She pulled out a chair and sat, burying her face in her hands.

Caleb knelt in front of her and peeled away her hands.

"Yes, Zoe, it does. Very much. It affects you, so it affects me. First of all, I was very wrong to jump to conclusions. I'm so sorry about that. As for Griffin—he may be upset by how they're treating his family, but he knows the truth about you, your family and Agape House. I have a feeling he will be your strongest defender."

"But at what cost? I just want to get in my car and go. Leave this town behind and start fresh elsewhere."

"Is that what you really want? To run again? Doesn't that get old?" Caleb picked up a shirt and started folding it. "What about Griffin? Your family? Me?"

"You're all better off without me."

He reached for another shirt and folded it. "So, tell me, Zoe, who do you have planning this party of yours?"

"What are you talking about? I'm not having a party."

"Your pity party. Sounds like you're hosting quite the shindig."

"Don't be ridiculous. And stop folding my clothes." She snatched the shirt away from him and tossed it on the couch.

"I'm not the one being ridiculous." He reached for the shirt again and refolded it. He dropped it on the couch, then waved a hand around the room, his voice raising. "This is ridiculous. Where's your faith, Zoe? Where's your fight?"

"I don't have any left." She dropped on the couch surrounded by her mess. "I'm tired of struggling."

"Your struggles are an important part of growing in your faith. Let me help fight for you."

"I'm not your problem."

Caleb reached for her hands and pulled her to him. He cradled her face in his hands. "I'm in love with you,

Zoe. I think I have been from the day you sewed Melly Moon's head back on."

"Then you're a fool. I have a past." She twisted her hands in the folds of his shirt. "This mess isn't even over. I have to go back to court. I could go back to prison, Sully."

"I'm not going to let that happen." He pressed her head against his chest and enfolded her in his embrace. "I love you despite your past. That's always going to be a part of you, but it doesn't define you. You're a beautiful woman with a young son who's spent too much time away from his mom. Instead of wanting to run away, face your Goliath. It takes only one stone to take down your giant."

She sighed, relaxing against him. "Where do I start? I don't want to be a disappointment anymore."

"You'll never be a disappointment to me. Your son adores you. My girls think the world of you. We are here with you, every step of the way." Caleb pulled back and cupped her face. "Before I came here, I drove out to the parking lot next to The Sassy Cat. There's a security camera overlooking that area. That footage will prove you weren't on Sassy Cat property."

"That wasn't my beer bottle."

"I believe you. Your attorney will be interviewing Gina and the bartender. He never served you. With the time stamp on the camera footage coordinating with your cell phone records, there's enough for the judge to consider tossing the case all together. I love you, Zoe, and I'll do whatever it takes to protect you. I'm not going anywhere, and I promise never to doubt you again."

"You're a great cop, Sully."

"It's my superpower."

She reached up and brushed the hair off his forehead. "I love you, too. You've seen me like no one else does. I've never had anyone like you on my side before. I choose you, Caleb. You are enough for me."

He loved the sound of that. Now all he needed to do was make it permanent.

Chapter Fifteen

Caleb had never thrown a birthday party before, but with Zoe by his side, he was learning he could do pretty much anything.

Pink, green, and lavender balloons bobbed against the ceiling and hung in the doorways. A pink tablecloth covered the dining table where party hats, noisemakers and treat bags waited for the girls' friends from church and Ava's preschool program.

He wandered into the kitchen where Zoe swirled pink frosting from a pastry bag onto the tops of vanilla cupcakes. He slid an arm around her waist and pressed a kiss below her ear. She smelled of sugar and cake batter.

She nudged him away. "Hey, no distracting the decorator. I have to finish these before Sarah comes back with the girls."

He swiped a fingerful of frosting from the bowl and licked it off his finger. "I can't believe Ava's going to be four. Hopefully this next year will be a lot smoother for her."

"She's had a lot happen in her young life, but she's resilient, Sully."

"Have I told you how amazing you are?" And to think a week ago, he almost lost her due to his own stupidity.

"Hmm, not in the last hour." She smiled at him over her shoulder.

"Well, then let me remedy that." He took the pastry bag from her and set it on the counter. He lowered his mouth and brushed a kiss across her lips. "Apparently I'm not the only one testing the frosting."

"Quality control, you know." She grinned and picked up the pastry bag. She finished the last cupcake, and then arranged them on the tray in the shape of a flower. "How's that?"

The woman constantly amazed him. "Perfect. She'll love it. Thank you."

"I enjoyed it."

"If you get tired of the dog business, you can always go into the cupcake business."

"Yes, that would be a pretty sweet line of work." She licked frosting off her finger, then carried everything to the sink and ran hot water into the bowl.

Riley barked and raced for the front door. Caleb pushed aside the kitchen curtain to see his sister pulling into the driveway. "Sarah's here. I'm going to give her a hand with the girls."

He headed out the front door and made it to the car as Sarah lifted a sleeping Ava out of her seat. Caleb unbuckled Ella. She struggled to open her eyes. Spying him, she smiled. "Hi, Daddy."

"Hi, chipmunk. Are you ready for a party?"

She nodded, but laid her head on his shoulder. For a moment he held her and allowed her sweetness to wrap around his heart. No matter what problems he had had this year, his daughters were turning out pretty okay.

He followed Sarah into the house and laid Ella on the couch at the opposite end from her sleeping sister. Instead of going back to sleep, she sat up and looked around, gathering her bearings. Ava opened her eyes, but didn't move.

Caleb sank onto the couch beside her and pushed her hair off her face. "Aves, your party will start in a little bit. Are you ready to wake up? Daddy and Zoe got you a very special present, but we want to give it to you now. Okay?"

She smiled and nodded. She crawled into his lap. He pulled off her fleece jacket, revealing a pink sweater and matching leggings.

Zoe carried a wriggling box covered in cartoon puppy dog wrapping paper and set it on the floor in front of Caleb and Ava.

She glanced at him with wide eyes as if to ask, "For me?"

He smiled and gave her a brief hug. "Yes, Aves, that's for you."

She touched the box, and it wiggled. She jerked back and hid her face in Caleb's shirt.

Caleb laughed. "It's okay, sweetheart. Maybe Ella can help us, too."

"Come on, Avie. I'll help you." Wearing a lime green sweater and leggings, Ella knelt on the floor by the box and opened the flaps.

Ava scooted off Caleb's lap and peered inside the box. She gasped, and then smiled. Caleb reached inside the box, lifted out a marshmallow-colored schnauzer, and held the trembling dog close to his chest. He turned to Ava. "His name is Shiloh."

Ella jumped up and extended her hand the way Zoe had taught them when she helped them train Riley. Shiloh sniffed her fingers, then Ella petted the dog's back. "Oh, Daddy. He's so cute, isn't he, Avie?"

Ava watched them with wide eyes and nodded. A huge smile spread across her face.

"Would you like to hold him?"

She nodded again and reached out her hand like Ella had done. Shiloh licked the tips of her fingers, causing her to giggle. She climbed up on the couch and sat beside Caleb.

He set the dog in her arms. Shiloh wiggled and tried to lick her face.

"He likes you, Aves."

Ava leaned back, hesitating, but then she reached out and stroked his fur with a finger. For several minutes she continued petting him, not taking her eyes off him. Once Shiloh settled in her lap, she hugged him and rested her cheek on his head. She looked up at Caleb with large eyes and whispered, "Fank you, Daddy."

Caleb's pulse quickened. Did she just...talk?

His eyes darted to Zoe and Sarah, who had been taking pictures. Everyone stopped, waiting and wondering.

"What was that, Ava? I couldn't hear you."

"I said 'Fank you, Daddy.' I love him."

Caleb slammed his eyelids shut and forced back the sudden gush of wetness. His chin quivered. He worked his jaw and swallowed the boulder in his throat. Once he could talk without bawling, he opened his eyes and ran a hand over her hair. "Oh, baby. I'm so glad. So glad."

With watery eyes, he peered at Sarah to see tears sliding silently down her cheeks. Her gaze connected with him, and she smiled.

Zoe watched them with tenderness in her eyes as she brushed away a tear with her fingertip. She crossed behind the couch and stood behind him, leaning down to kiss his cheek. She pressed her lips close to his ear and whispered, "You're an amazing man and a terrific dad, Caleb Sullivan."

He threaded his fingers through hers and kissed her knuckles as his heart swelled with emotion.

Thank you, Lord.

His sweet Ava had finally broken from her own darkness. Had he not met Zoe and her love for animals, who knew how long it would be before Ava came out of her shell?

He'd made many mistakes and would probably continue to do so, but for the first time in his life, he knew he could handle the big stuff and the little things as long as he had Zoe by his side. Now he just needed to find the right time to ask her to be a part of their lives.

From the moment Sully and his daughters entered her life, things hadn't been the same. And Zoe wouldn't have it any other way. She planned to spend every day of the rest of their lives letting them know how special they were to her.

Dad, Ian and Sully, with Riley napping on his lap, lounged in front of the TV in Mom and Dad's living room, watching a football game. Amos, Mom and Dad's golden retriever, curled up in his bed near the fireplace, sleeping in spite of the noise.

Mom, Agnes and Mary, Agnes's mom, talked in the kitchen over cups of tea. With Harper and Shiloh at his feet, Griffin entertained Ella and Ava at the cleared dining room table with a game of Candy Land.

With dishes done and food put away after their traditional Sunday dinner, Zoe wrapped an afghan around her shoulders and headed out to the back deck. She stretched out on one of the cushioned loungers, threw her arm over her head and sighed. The scent of wood smoke drifted through the chilly air.

The bare branches above her head swayed as the late afternoon wind blew, ruffling her hair and scattering leaves off the neatly raked piles. The chill nipped at her nose and cheeks, but Zoe made no move to head back inside.

With seven adults, three kids and four dogs, she needed a couple of minutes of solitude. She'd really like a nap, but if she stayed outside, she'd turn into a Popsicle. She burrowed her chin into the collar of her fisherman's sweater and tightened the blanket around her arms. Closing her eyes for a minute, she released a contented sigh.

She was blessed. Definitely blessed.

With the drama of her recent arrest behind her, she was able to focus on building a life with Griffin now that the courts had awarded her custody over the Jacobys. Mom had mentioned that the house seemed so quiet now that Griffin was living with Zoe, but they still spent plenty of time with her parents.

She was finally free from the shackles of her old life, thanks to God's grace and mercy. And Sully's love. She was so undeserving, but incredibly grateful.

The French doors opened, allowing a burst of noise from the living room to intrude on her quiet, but she didn't mind.

She expected Mom to come out and check on her, so when Dad stepped out onto the deck carrying a rectangular package wrapped in kraft paper, she was a little surprised.

"Mind if I join you, or would you prefer to be alone?"

She waved a hand to the matching lounger. "Pull up a chair, but don't expect much of a tan."

Dad chuckled as he sat on the edge of the chair. He rubbed his hands together and blew into them. "Forecast is calling for a dusting of snow this weekend."

"Crazy, huh?"

"Hope you don't plan on staying out here too long."

"No, not really. Just needed a few quiet minutes."

"Would you like me to leave you alone?"

"No, stay. Please."

The lounger creaked as Dad moved into a more comfortable position.

For a moment, silence settled over them like a cozy blanket. Zoe closed her eyes again and listened to a barn owl in one of the high branches.

"Zoe, I have something for you."

She turned her head and popped open one eye to look at him, but made no move to leave her comfortable spot. "What is it?"

"Open it and find out." He handed the package to her.

Zoe swung her legs around and sat up, keeping the afghan wrapped tightly around her. The package weighed very little in her hands. She turned it over, slid her finger under the tape and peeled back the brown paper, exposing the back of a stretched canvas and releasing the faint scent of paint.

She flipped the canvas over and gasped. Her hand flew to her mouth as she stared at the painting through a sheen of tears. "Dad…"

The butterfly painting that hung above the fireplace at Agape House. *Mon Petit Papillon*—My Tiny Butterfly. Zoe traced the wings of the butterfly. "I was afraid of the butterflies that day, but you promised you'd walk beside me and protect me."

Clearing his throat, Dad rested his elbows on his knees and rubbed his hands together. "I haven't lived up to that promise, Zoe, and for that I'm sorry."

Zoe realized he wasn't talking about that specific day, but in general. "Dad—"

He held up a hand. "Let me finish. I thought I was showing tough love, but I ended up turning my back on you when you needed me most. I can't go back and undo the choices I've made, but I will promise never to abandon or reject you again. I'm sorry."

Since her return home, Zoe had longed to reestablish her relationship with her dad, especially after seeing the way Sully cared for Ella and Ava. But she knew it would take time, so she didn't push it. And the reward was sweeter than she could have imagined.

Dad stood and then sat beside her. He reached for her hand. "When you came to Agape House, I was convinced you wouldn't change because I watched my parents lose the battle with alcohol time and time again. But you've proved me wrong. You've worked hard to be responsible and trustworthy. I'm so proud of you. I love you."

A new batch of tears bathed her eyes. She threw her arms around his neck and hugged him. "I love you, too, Dad. Thank you for not giving up on me, even when I was really struggling. I promise never to hurt any of you like that again."

Dad sniffed, crushed her against his chest and kissed the top of her head. "I know. I believe in you. You know, for a butterfly, struggling is an important part of their growing experience. The struggle is what causes them to develop their wings to fly."

"I'm definitely ready to fly."

He released her and picked up the canvas. "I didn't have it framed because I didn't know what kind of wood or what color you'd like. Pick out your choice, and I'll take care of it for you."

Zoe wiped her eyes with her sleeve. "Thanks, Dad."

"Let's get out of this cold before we both freeze and see if your mom will let us cut into the pie yet." He stood and extended a hand.

Zoe grabbed the paper and the painting, then placed her hand in his calloused one, his warmth spreading up her arm, and stood. She wrapped her arms around his waist for another hug, releasing years of longing and soaking in a lifetime of love.

Dad reached for the afghan and settled an arm around her shoulders. He opened the door, and the heat and the lingering scents from dinner smacked them in the face as they left the cold behind and embraced the warmth of family.

Caleb couldn't remember the last time he'd been so nervous. Even though he kept his eyes focused on the TV, he couldn't recall any of the plays. His insides wobbled like Jell-O.

The sliding glass door opened, and Zoe entered with her father. Caleb pushed to his feet. He needed to talk to her now before he lost his nerve.

He reached her and breathed in the scent of fresh air that swirled around her. Cupping her elbow, he leaned close and whispered, "Hey, you got a minute? I need to talk to you about something."

She frowned. "Everything okay?"

"Yes, most definitely." More than okay. He nodded toward the door. "Mind if we sit outside for a minute?"

"Sure."

Caleb opened the door and stepped back for her to pass by. His legs threatened to give out on him. But he could do this. The love he felt for Zoe helped him to know he was making the right decision.

Zoe kept the afghan around her shoulders and leaned against the railing. Her beautiful hair had been piled in a jumble of curls on her head, showcasing her elegant neck.

He jammed his hands into his pockets and wrapped his fingers around the box he'd had for a couple of weeks.

The glow of the full moon fell over her, making her look even more beautiful, if that was possible. He reached out and stroked her cheek with his finger. "You're beautiful."

She lowered her eyes as her lips tipped into a smile. "Thanks, you're not so hard on the eyes yourself. You okay?"

"Yes, why?"

"You seem…I don't know…a little antsy or something."

He tried to hide it, but Zoe picked up on everything.

Caleb gathered her chilled hands in his and brushed his thumbs over her fingers, long and delicate. "Zoe, I love you."

"I love you, too."

"I know we haven't been together as a couple that long, but when you came back into my life, I knew God was giving me…giving us a fresh start. Your determination and gentle strength amaze me every day. The love you show my daughters is more than any father could ask for." He released her hands, reached into his pocket and pulled out a black velvet box. Easing down on one knee in front of her, he opened the box.

The moonlight sparkled over the white-gold, princess-cut diamond engagement ring resting in a bed of ivory satin. "I've talked to Griffin and the girls. I've asked your dad for his blessing. So now, it's all up to you—Zoe James, will you do me the honor of becoming my wife?"

A hand flew to her mouth as she gasped. Tears filled her eyes, and she nodded. "Yes, Caleb Sullivan, of course."

He took the ring out of the box and slid it onto her trembling finger. Perfect fit. He stood, gathered her in his arms and kissed her. He had finally found a place where he belonged—forever in her heart.

* * * * *

Dear Reader,

When I pitched the idea of Zoe's story to my editor, I was quite surprised when she offered me the contract, because Zoe spent time in prison. When I shared that with her, she said, "God can redeem anyone."

In *Lakeside Redemption*, Zoe longs to find redemption from her past shame—her choices took someone's life. She carries that burden daily. How could God love someone like her? She struggles to embrace God's amazing love and redemption in spite of her past sins. Caleb longs for a fresh start after his wife walked out on their family and a tragedy at work caused him to lose his partner and his career as he knew it. Zoe and Caleb realize God's redemption sets them free to explore the new direction He has for their lives.

We all have those dark moments in our lives that may keep us from accepting God's redeeming grace. Despite our flaws and scars, God loves us unconditionally. He offers us a gift of grace that is ours only for the taking. When we embrace His redemptive grace, we are offered new directions for our lives, too. May you embrace His grace to have the life He's envisioned for you.

I love to hear from my readers, so visit me at www.lisajordanbooks.com or email me at lisa@lisajordanbooks.com!

Embracing His grace,

Lisa Jordan

Questions for Discussion

1. Zoe James and Caleb Sullivan haven't seen each other since college ten years ago. Their rekindled friendship sparks a deeper relationship. Have you ever become reacquainted with a friend from your past? How did it work out?

2. Caleb Sullivan lost his wife, his partner and his career. Yet those losses are what gave him the greatest gain—a new life in Christ. Share how a dark time in your life brought you closer to Christ.

3. Zoe longs to be the kind of mother her son deserves. What piece of advice would you offer Zoe?

4. Caleb and his daughters adopt Riley from Canine Companions. Have you ever adopted a pet from a shelter? How did it work out for you?

5. Zoe loves animals. She feels training dogs is her superpower. What is your superpower? What are you good at doing?

6. When Caleb learns about Zoe's past, he's conflicted. After all, his wife was an alcoholic who chose the bottle over her family. Share a time when you were conflicted about a difficult situation and how you solved it.

7. Zoe's relationship with her dad is shaky. He said he forgave her, but she wonders if he really feels it

in his heart where it matters. Have you struggled with a relationship with a loved one? How did you work it out?

8. Zoe's friend Gina struggles after leaving Agape House. She feels her old friends offer her more grace than the people in her church. Why do you think that is?

9. Griffin wants to live with his mom and be a real family. What is your definition of a "real family"?

10. After Zoe's arrest, she wants to leave town because she feels trapped. Have you ever felt trapped where you live? What advice would you have for Zoe?

11. Caleb is a cop who has fallen in love with an ex-convict. He struggles with what others will think, but then realizes that's in her past. God's grace redeems us from past shames. Share how God's grace has enabled you to move on from your past shames.

12. Zoe has a lot to be thankful for—a healed relationship with her dad, a man who loves her in spite of her past and a new blended family. What are you most thankful for?

COMING NEXT MONTH FROM
Love Inspired®

Available January 20, 2015

A MATCH FOR ADDY
The Amish Matchmaker • by Emma Miller

Addy Coblentz and Gideon Esch are looking for love—just not with each other. But soon the unlikely pair discover their perfect match is right before their eyes.

DADDY WANTED
by Renee Andrews

When Claremont's wild child Savvy Bowers returns to care for her friend's orphaned children, she finds a home in the town she once rejected—and the man who once betrayed her.

HOMETOWN VALENTINE
Moonlight Cove • by Lissa Manley

Unexpected dad Blake Stonely needs a nanny—fast! When caretaker Lily Rogers comes to the rescue, can this caring beauty also mend his broken heart?

THE FIREMAN'S SECRET
Goose Harbor • by Jessica Keller

Fireman Joel Palermo has put his rebellious youth behind him. But when his return to Goose Harbor reveals his mistakes left Shelby Beck scarred forever, can he ever gain her forgiveness and her love?

HEALING THE WIDOWER'S HEART
by Susan Anne Mason

Seeking help for his troubled son, minister Nathan Porter makes a desperate plea to Paige McFarlane. But when her soothing words begin to heal his *own* heart, soon he's falling for the pretty counselor.

FALLING FOR TEXAS
by Jill Lynn

When teacher Olivia Grayson teams up with rancher Cash Maddox to keep his teenage sister on the right track, their promise to stay *just* friends is put to the ultimate test.

LICNM0115

REQUEST YOUR FREE BOOKS!

2 FREE INSPIRATIONAL NOVELS
PLUS 2
FREE
MYSTERY GIFTS

Love Inspired

YES! Please send me 2 FREE Love Inspired® novels and my 2 FREE mystery gifts (gifts are worth about $10). After receiving them, if I don't wish to receive any more books, I can return the shipping statement marked "cancel." If I don't cancel, I will receive 6 brand-new novels every month and be billed just $4.74 per book in the U.S. or $5.24 per book in Canada. That's a saving of at least 21% off the cover price. It's quite a bargain! Shipping and handling is just 50¢ per book in the U.S. and 75¢ per book in Canada.* I understand that accepting the 2 free books and gifts places me under no obligation to buy anything. I can always return a shipment and cancel at any time. Even if I never buy another book, the two free books and gifts are mine to keep forever.

105/305 IDN F47Y

Name _____ (PLEASE PRINT)

Address _____ Apt. #

City _____ State/Prov. _____ Zip/Postal Code

Signature (if under 18, a parent or guardian must sign)

Mail to the Harlequin® Reader Service:
IN U.S.A.: P.O. Box 1867, Buffalo, NY 14240-1867
IN CANADA: P.O. Box 609, Fort Erie, Ontario L2A 5X3

**Are you a subscriber to Love Inspired books
and want to receive the larger-print edition?
Call 1-800-873-8635 or visit www.ReaderService.com.**

* Terms and prices subject to change without notice. Prices do not include applicable taxes. Sales tax applicable in N.Y. Canadian residents will be charged applicable taxes. Offer not valid in Quebec. This offer is limited to one order per household. Not valid for current subscribers to Love Inspired books. All orders subject to credit approval. Credit or debit balances in a customer's account(s) may be offset by any other outstanding balance owed by or to the customer. Please allow 4 to 6 weeks for delivery. Offer available while quantities last.

Your Privacy—The Harlequin® Reader Service is committed to protecting your privacy. Our Privacy Policy is available online at www.ReaderService.com or upon request from the Harlequin Reader Service.

We make a portion of our mailing list available to reputable third parties that offer products we believe may interest you. If you prefer that we not exchange your name with third parties, or if you wish to clarify or modify your communication preferences, please visit us at www.ReaderService.com/consumerchoice or write to us at Harlequin Reader Service Preference Service, P.O. Box 9062, Buffalo, NY 14269. Include your complete name and address.

LI13R

SPECIAL EXCERPT FROM

Love Inspired®

*A young Amish woman is rescued from a thorny briar
bush by a mysterious stranger.*

*Read on for a preview of A MATCH FOR ADDY
by Emma Miller, the first book in her new series,*
THE AMISH MATCHMAKER.

"Are you hurt?"

Dorcas froze. She didn't recognize this stranger's voice. Frantically, she attempted to cover her bare shins. "I'm caught," she squeaked out. "My dress…"

"*Ne, maedle*, lie still."

She squinted at him in the sunshine. This was no lad, but a young man. She clamped her eyes shut, hoping the ground would swallow her up.

She felt the tension on her dress suddenly loosen.

"There you go."

Before she could protest, he was lifting her out of the briars.

He cradled her against him. "Best I get you to Sara and have her take a look at that knee. Might need stitches." He started to walk across the field toward Sara's.

Dorcas looked into a broad, shaven face framed by shaggy butter-blond hair that hung almost to his wide shoulders. He was the most attractive man she had ever laid eyes on. He was too beautiful to be real, this man with merry pewter-gray eyes and suntanned skin.

I must have hit the post with my head and knocked myself silly, she thought.

"I can…" She pushed against his shoulders, thinking she should walk.

"*Ne*, you could do yourself more harm." He shifted her weight. "You'll be more comfortable if you put your arms around my neck."

"I…I…" she mumbled, but she did as he said. She knew that this was improper, but she couldn't figure out what to do.

"You must be the little cousin Sara said was coming to help her today," he said. "I'm Gideon Esch, her hired man. From Wisconsin."

Little? She was five foot eleven, a giant compared to most of the local women. No one had ever called her *little* before.

"You don't say much, do you?" He looked down at her in his arms and grinned.

Dorcas nodded.

He grinned. "I like you. Do you have a name?"

"Dorcas. Dorcas Coblentz."

"You don't look like a Dorcas to me."

He stopped walking to look down at her. "I don't suppose you have a middle name?"

"Adelaide."

"Adelaide," he repeated. "Addy. You look a lot more like an Addy than you do a Dorcas."

"Addy?" The idea settled over her as easily as warm maple syrup over blueberry pancakes. "Addy," she repeated, and then she found herself smiling back at him.

Will Addy fall for the handsome Amish handyman?
Pick up A MATCH FOR ADDY to find out!
Available February 2015,
wherever Love Inspired® books and ebooks are sold.

SPECIAL EXCERPT FROM

Love Inspired.
SUSPENSE

A woman's young son has gone missing.
Can he be found?

Read on for a preview of *TO SAVE HER CHILD*
by Margaret Daley, the next book in her
ALASKAN SEARCH AND RESCUE series.

"What's wrong, Ella?" Josiah's dark blue eyes filled with concern.

Words stuck in her throat. She fought the tears welling in her. "My son is missing," she finally squeaked out.

"Where? When?" he asked, suddenly all business.

"About an hour ago at Camp Yukon. I hope you can help look for him."

"Let's go. My truck is outside." Josiah fell into step next to her.

Ella slid a glance toward him, and the sight of Josiah, a former US marine, calmed her nerves. She knew how good he was with his dog at finding people. Robbie would be all right. She had to believe that. The alternative was unthinkable.

He opened the back door for his dog, Buddy, then quickly moved to the front door for Ella. "I'll find Robbie. I promise."

The confidence in his voice further eased her anxiety. Ella climbed into the cab with Josiah's hand on her elbow.

As he started the engine, Ella ran her hands up and down her arms. But the chill burrowed its way into the marrow of her bones, even though the temperature was sixty-five.

Josiah glanced at her. "David will get plenty of people to scour the whole park. Do you have anything with Robbie's scent on it?"

"I do. In my car."

He backed up to her black Jeep Wrangler. "Where?"

"Front seat. A jacket he didn't take with him."

Josiah jumped out of the truck to get it before Ella had a chance to even open her door.

He returned quickly with Robbie's brown jacket in his grasp.

He gave it to Ella. "This will help Buddy find your son."

Ella leaned forward, staring out the windshield at the sky. Dark clouds drifted over the sun. "Looks like we'll have a storm late this afternoon."

Josiah's strong jawline twitched. "We can still search in the rain, but let's hope that the weatherman is wrong."

Ella closed her eyes. She had to remain calm and in control. That was one of the things she'd always been able to do in the middle of a search and rescue, but this time it was her son.

"Ella, I promise you," Josiah said. "I won't leave the park until we find your son."

Will Robbie be found before nightfall?
Pick up TO SAVE HER CHILD to find out.
Available February 2015, wherever
Love Inspired® Suspense books and ebooks are sold.